THE
Worlds
THAT
Separated
US

Cover & Interior Design by Stone Ridge Books

ISBN 978-1-8383491-0-3 (paperback)
ISBN 978-1-8383491-1-0 (ebook)

For more information contact:
Light and Joy Publishing Ltd.
Unit 508
Moat House
54 Bloomfield Avenue
Belfast
BT5 5AD

10 9 8 7 6 5 4 3 2 1

THE Worlds THAT Separated US

MEGAN JAYNE

Light and Joy

PUBLISHING LTD.

For Christopher

Chapter 1

Her hands pressed tight over my eyes as she guided me into the brisk air, the raised tone to her voice giving away her excitement.

'One ... Two ... Three, you can open your eyes now Rosie!' Mum dropped her hand onto my shoulder and squeezed. Her smile lit her face, as the corners of her eyes creased the wrinkles folded together. Her eyes twinkled in delight as they drifted from me toward a black Ford Focus with a large vibrant red bow tied neatly to the bonnet.

'What? No Way!' I gasped, wrapping my arms around her, pulling her in close.

'Happy graduation,' Dad pressed his hand against my arm, before rattling a set of keys. I reached up as he set them into my hand and placed a kiss on his cheek. 'Thank you, Dad.' I smiled, clutching the keys in my palm.

'Your dad has been working on this one for months,' Mum beamed.

Dad works as the Construction Director for a local building firm, although he likes to dabble with rebuilding cars in his spare time. It has turned into quite the hobby for him. As soon as he gets home from work, he slips into overalls and heads out to our garage for hours. The music from his vintage record player drifts through our kitchen window, and his taste in music is something I share.

'Thank you, thank you, thank you.' I ran my fingers over the scratched paintwork, hesitating when I reached the handle to the driver's side.

'Come on, let's take it on a test drive.' Caleb opened the passenger door, taking a seat, he instantly began pressing and twisting each button on the dash. I looked over my shoulder checking my mum and dad were ok with Caleb's request, when Mum gave me an approving nod, I pulled open the door.

'Don't be away too long, we don't want to be late for the ceremony,' Dad's face was serious for a moment before relaxing, the sides of his white moustache twisted upwards into a smile.

I rested my hands around the steering wheel keeping my grip loose, letting them drift along the curves until meeting again in the middle, the leather cold against my skin. As I twisted the keys starting the engine the car jutted forward and stalled. I caught Caleb smirking and lifted one finger toward him, 'Don't.' I warned as red began to bloom along my cheeks. He held his hands up innocently, not saying a word, then reached to the radio turning it back on and flicking through station after station until he found his favourite. The only one he would ever entertain listening to. I started up the engine a second time, this time making sure the gear stick was in neutral. I waved to our parents as I pulled out of the driveway into the street. Caleb drummed his hand along the window and bobbed his head to the music that was now too loud to talk over. I drove through the streets of our familiar town, nestled away in the Highlands.

I reached over pressing on the volume button to lower it so Caleb could hear me, 'did you know about this?'

'Maybe.' He ran his fingers through his messy blond hair and smirked at me.

'Do you think Mum and Dad would ever forgive us if we missed the ceremony?' I raised my eyebrow, teasing with the idea. I knew it wouldn't take much convincing for Caleb; he was already being forced against his will to attend. Although I couldn't deal with the inevitable wrath our parents would bring down on us if I skipped my own graduation. Caleb toyed with the idea, before we both agreed to return home, neither of us realizing we were already running late.

I slipped into the dress mum and I picked out a few weeks ago, the emerald green chiffon fabric floated just above my knee covering a small childhood scar. I had loved this dress from the moment I first laid my eyes on it, it was perfect. It brought out the green in my eyes, contrasting against my pale complexion and hugging my curves. I gently pinned back pieces of my long brown curly hair, making sure my face was free from any unruly strands. Adding some light makeup and applying some berry lipstick to complete my look. I took one final glance in the floor length mirror that rested against my lilac bedroom wall, smoothing down the fabric of my dress. I hurried downstairs to meet the rest of my family. As I reached the landing I peeked over the banister, my dad leaned against the wall staring at the gold watch that hung a little loose around his wrist, as Mum impatiently tapped her foot against the hard wood flooring her gaze fixated on the staircase. Mum hated the very thought of being late and yet I don't remember the last time we arrived early or even at the right time to any event. With Caleb usually the culprit, today I filled those shoes and I'm not so sure I like the warning look in my mother's eye. I hadn't even made it to the last stair before Mum swung open the front door allowing the cold air to clash with heat from the hallway. I was going to suggest going in Caleb's car, then thought better of it, opting to travel with my parents instead. Caleb following closely behind alone in his car, while I tried my best to appease Mum.

When we arrived my parents and Caleb rushed off to their seats as I collected my cap and gown, I found Libby along the rows and rows of other students her distinctive auburn hair poked out from under her cap and gave her away. I excused myself as I pushed past a few familiar faces to take the seat beside her, she had rested her handbag there to keep it for me.

'Thanks Libs,' she moved her bag back into her lap as I took a seat.

'I can't believe we are graduating today!' Libby shrieked.

I nodded in response, unsure of what words to conjure as a reply. She has been my best friend ever since we were little, I can't remember a time without her. We've always done everything together, now everything's going to change. Libby, unlike me, has always been sure of herself and what she wanted to do. She's going to be a nurse like her mother and her grandmother before her, following in their footsteps. Me on the other hand, I've never known. I studied Modern Art however I'm not sure that's what I'm really passionate about. Libby already has a job lined up and I haven't thought that far ahead yet. Maybe I'm not a planner or maybe I'm procrastinating, but either way I need to make a decision, I can't work at the local restaurant for the rest of my life. Right now though, I'm going to try my best to enjoy this day. I had been so busy worrying about my future that I had completely forgotten I was next to take the stage when the announcer called my name.

'Rosie Paterson.'

I stood up readjusting my gown carefully and checked that my cap was still in its place. I took a step out into the centre aisle and realised this is it. The end of my education. Suddenly the thought of the steps and my heels occurred to me. I walked carefully toward the stage, trying my best not to fall. I took my time walking up each step, making sure to pay careful attention to my footing. I shook the announcer's hand, pausing for a photo, and then went quickly to where my family were sitting, allowing my mum to gush and take as many photos as she wanted. Dad at this stage was just as enthusiastic as Mum, Caleb on the other hand, had fallen asleep. His head was slouched down into his chest, and a faint purring sounded from his nose. I chuckled at the sight of him, I can't say I blame him, graduation ceremonies are boring. His was just two years ago and if I could have gotten comfortable enough, I would have slept through it as well. We gathered our things once the rest of the ceremony was over. Libby had somehow convinced her parents to let her go with us, which didn't surprise me at all. She has always been able to talk her way out of things.

'Come on, Let's go,' she grabbed hold of my hand pulling me in the direction of Caleb's car. We were headed straight to my favourite place to eat, which happened to be the same restaurant I work at, Sleepy Thistle. Not to mention it is the only restaurant in our small town.

'So, Caleb ...' I asked, grinning.

'Yes, Rosie?' he raised his eyebrow and glanced back at me in the rear-view mirror.

'Did you enjoy the ceremony?'

'Ahh ... yeah, it was good.' He looked over to Libby who had tilted her body around in her seat so she could look between us crossing her arms as an amused glint shun in her eyes.

'Tell me which part was your *favourite?*'

'My favourite part ... let's see,' he drummed his fingers along his chin dramatically, 'Ahh yes, it was definitely the part when we left.'

Caleb chuckled, as Libby and I joined in. We laughed and continued chatting until we reached the restaurant. Caleb left the car first and opened my door before walking to Libby's to do the same. He was always such a gentleman, which is probably why he could get away with anything.

I pressed my hands against the metal bar on the glass door pushing against it to open. The aroma of the food filled the air, I inhaled taking in all the familiar scents. I was almost able to tell what everyone in the restaurant was eating just by the smell. It was the knowledge I obtained from working here for almost three years. It didn't matter that the menu hadn't been changed in that time, the food was incredible, and I'm yet to try something that rivals it. It's simplistic, more fast food than restaurant quality and that's exactly why I like it. I hung my coat on the freestanding coat rack that stood beside the entrance, Caleb and Libby followed behind me as I made my way over to Piper. She gave me a friendly smile, her bright pink hair rested in a bun on top of her head.

'Your parents are already over there.' Piper pointed to the table under the window, I peered past her to my parents and rolled my eyes at her as she giggled. Mum refuses to sit anywhere else, and I've never understood her need to look at a car park whilst eating.

'Congratulations by the way,' she smiled.

'Thanks, is Kane working?' I asked as she handed me three tattered menus.

'Yeah, he's out the back on a smoking break. You want me to go get him?' She turned her head away to peek into the kitchen.

'No, it's ok. Do you know if the rota for next week is up yet?'

She shook her head, 'No, he said it'll be up later tonight though, I asked him earlier.'

'I'll text him later then, thanks.'

'Right Rosie come on let's get going I'm starving!' Caleb groaned from behind me.

'Ok, ok, sorry.' I gave an apologetic smile to Piper before making my way over to the table, I was about to take my seat when the door to the restaurant chimed open, and my eyes locked with his, *Greyson*. He smiled as he made his way closer to me. We've been together for a little under a year and he is perfect. I mean it, he is literally perfect. He is stereotypically tall dark and handsome; his brown eyes and hair complement his dark complexion and muscular build. Sometimes I can't believe he is mine. We met the day Caleb invited him over to our house, they were on the same rugby team together in university. I liked him from that moment, I couldn't believe when I found out he felt the same about me. Me, Libby, Caleb, and Greyson used to go everywhere together, until Grey and I started dating and Caleb started acting weird. Their friendship became strained after that. I told Grey that if he just wanted us to continue as friends, I'd be ok with it. We tried and failed miserably. We couldn't stay away from each other and we've been together ever since. I never doubt how lucky I am to have him in my life, though I can't help missing the days when it was the four of us.

'Congratulations,' he said while passing me a small carefully wrapped gift. I untied the white ribbon surrounding it and tore gently at the paper to reveal a smooth black velvet box. I looked at Grey as my smile grew wider in anticipation, his hand rested carefully on my waist, waiting patiently for me to open it.

I pushed open the lid of the tiny box and exhaled, 'It's beautiful, thank you so much.'

I removed a long silver necklace with a delicate blue stone that glistened in the natural light penetrating through the windows of the restaurant. He took the necklace from my hands into his and gestured for me to turn. Tenderly he brushed my hair over my shoulder and fastened the necklace in place, lowering his head to place a soft kiss on my neck.

'Let's order,' Caleb interrupted, pushing past Greyson.

We took our seats and turned to look closely at the menu, I don't even know why I look at it, I have it memorized. I guess it's just out of habit.

'So, Rosie, we haven't discussed your plans,' Dad broke the silence.

I could feel everyone looking at me without having to look up from the menu. Dad had been giving me until graduation to make up my mind about my future career and he held his end of the bargain. He promised he wouldn't mention it until I graduated. I should have known he wouldn't wait around too long to bring it up. He wants me to join his construction company. Caleb studied to become an architect in university, so as soon as he graduated, he became Dad's go to man. I on the other hand have no experience with the building trade and neither do I want it. Though he gave me an ultimatum, either I find a job – a real job, or I work for him as his office assistant, sorting his accounts and handling his clientele. Being stuck in an office all day is the last thing I want to do. I'd take waitressing over that any day, but how can I let him down? It's not like our town exactly has many opportunities for a Modern Art major. What was my choice, really?

'I haven't decided yet,' I answered him honestly.

'Well we did say graduation, perhaps you should give my proposal a second thought?' he took a sip of his water and looked to me waiting for my reply.

I knew exactly what Dad was trying to do, pressure me into it in front of everyone. He's good, though he is also right, it really is my only option right now.

'I'll think about it.'

'Good, that's all I'm asking. You need to start thinking about your long-term future. You're twenty-one now after all, your mother and I only want the best for you, you need a real job with a real income. You aren't going to want to live at home forever, are you? Well unless you're like your brother, I don't think we are ever going to get rid of him,' Dad joked.

'Hey! The problem is you're too cheap on rent,' Caleb smirked.

'Libby, any chance you can take him off our hands?'

'I keep trying but he won't budge,' Libby laughed,

she reached beside her to Caleb's arm and nudged him playfully.

She wasn't lying, she had asked Caleb many times over the last few months to get a place with her in town. She had even gone so far as to drag me along to look at a few apartments with her in hopes that when she showed Caleb, he would change his mind. For some odd reason though, he wouldn't budge, he showed no interest at all at the potential properties, which for someone who seemed so serious with his girlfriend didn't add up. He was in a well-paid job and Libby was starting hers in a few weeks. It didn't make sense, but then again, a lot of what Caleb does doesn't make sense.

'I guess our last hope is Greyson taking Rosie off our hands?' Dad tilted his water glass gesturing toward Greyson, and shook his head laughing.

Grey gave me a playful smile and answered, 'Someday.'

My heart picked up pace at his comment, the thought of a someday with Greyson was enough for me. At least he wouldn't be as hard to convince as Caleb to move out, Libby's going to need to drag him by his heels kicking and screaming out of that house.

Caleb rolled his eyes at hearing Greyson's comment, he

really does hate that we are a couple and he certainly doesn't hide it. A future with Grey seems like the only thing I'm sure off. It does make Dad's proposition seem more appealing. If I took the job Greyson and I could have our own place in a few years. I could see myself settled with him, and I know he can see it too.

'I'll pick you up tomorrow after work,' Grey spoke as he walked me to Caleb's car.

He lent in about to kiss me goodnight when Caleb yelled for me to get going. I rolled my eyes and Greyson laughed opting to leave a quick kiss on my forehead instead. I hopped into the backseat of Caleb's car; Libby perched in the front holding Caleb's hand on her lap. I don't know why he is so touchy with me and Grey since he's been dating my best friend for the last two years, what is it to him if I'm dating his best friend? We pulled up to Libby's house and Caleb got out to walk her to her door. I jumped into the front seat for the journey home, taking my phone out to text Greyson whilst I waited for Caleb to say his long goodnight to Libby; I shook my head at his hypocrisy.

Rosie: Thanks for coming tonight.

Greyson: Wouldn't miss it. I'm proud of you, I love you. See you tomorrow.

Rosie: I can't wait, love you too.

Nice to know someone was proud of me for graduating. Caleb called my degree a 'waste of time and resources,' he meant it as a joke, but my dad agreed with him. The only people that seemed to think Modern Art was a good idea were Greyson and Libby. My mum stayed tight lipped on the subject, never wanting to rock the boat. I guess they were right though, although I'm good at art and it comes naturally to me, it's not exactly a career I can pursue here in this town, which brings me to the same crossroads Dad put me at earlier. Caleb got back into the car and drove off, we stayed in silence until we reached the house. As soon as we got inside, we set about to our usual routine of turning on the TV to watch a late-night movie.

'Popcorn?' Caleb asked.

'Why do you even ask that anymore? You know the answer.'

'Popcorn it is then.'

He made his way to the kitchen to grab the bag we kept stashed for nights like this. I was mad at him for how he acted back in the carpark of the restaurant. Caleb can be so stubborn, sometimes too much for his own good and I wasn't letting him get away easy this time. Greyson never wanted me to get involved so up until now I have stayed quiet. He always said it's his problem and he'll handle it then nothing ever gets resolved. It's gone on for long enough and what better a night than tonight for me to corner Caleb. He arrived back to the room with a large bowl filled to the brim with popcorn and chocolate mixed together. I waited for him to sit down and start flicking through the list of different film options, when he turned to ask me my opinion on his choice, I moved to face him.

'Why do you always do that with Grey?'

'What do you mean?' he shrugged away my question.

'You know what I mean Caleb,' I gave him a knowing glance.

'It's ... It's just weird for me when you kiss my best friend,' he stumbled on his words. He pushed back his blond hair and rested his hand on the back of his neck, looking up at me with his piercing green eyes. He looked paler than usual and awkward, like he was uncomfortable, which is out of character for Caleb. He's always so confident and never one to shy away from confrontation.

'You're my sister, and you can do better than Grey,' he laughed, trying to lighten the tense mood that now surrounded us. He turned his eyes back to the TV, wanting my interrogation to stop.

'Better than your best friend? Why would you even say that? You know how happy I am with him,' I could feel the anger start to pulse in my veins.

'I didn't mean it like that, and you know it,' he spoke defensively.

'What way was I meant to take it then Caleb? You have been going out with my best friend for almost two years and you never hear me complain or tell you there's someone better out there for you.'

'Rosie—'

'Stop, I don't want to hear it, I love him. I'm happy and it would be really great for both of us if you would just accept it. We aren't planning on breaking up any time soon, so you'd better just learn to get over yourself,' I stood up ready to leave.

'You have no idea,' he muttered under his breath.

'You are so selfish, are you the only one that's allowed to be happy? You might be my older brother, but I don't need your protection anymore.'

'I'm selfish, seriously. You really have no clue what you are even talking about.'

'Then please enlighten me,' I opened my arms gesturing for him to continue.

Caleb looked away avoiding eye contact with me, focusing again on the TV. After no response I chose to ignore him and leave before our argument escalated any more than it already had. He's my brother, he means so much to me, I just wish he would accept that me and Grey are together. Greyson rarely mentions it, but I can tell not having Caleb's approval gets to him. Caleb's always been there for me through everything, protecting me. It just really tears me apart that he chooses this to fight with me over. He has distanced himself from Greyson since we got together, it's obvious our relationship is the reason. Caleb wants us to break up and he's made it more than evident on multiple occasions that he won't be fully happy until then. That will never happen.

Chapter 2

A few days passed without Caleb and I talking, I hated not speaking to him, but he needed to know how serious I was.

'Rosie, Greyson's here for you,' Dad shouted from downstairs. I finished putting on my makeup and grabbed my weekend bag from on top of my still unmade bed.

'You ready?' Greyson smiled, taking my bag from my grasp. He had booked a small lakeside cabin for us for the weekend after my graduation, and we both couldn't wait. A few days away from everything, and everyone.

'Yes,' I replied almost screaming with excitement.

'Enjoy yourselves,' Mum shouted after us.

'Don't forget to call when you get there.' Dad added.

I jumped in the passenger seat whilst Greyson packed up his car. I had maybe overpacked just a little for two days, but like Libby always says, you can never be too prepared, I think she's rubbed off on me. Greyson and I have never been alone together for this long so the thought of spending a weekend uninterrupted with him is a welcomed change.

The hours spent on the road flew by, spending time with Greyson has that effect. It's so easy with him; we have so many of the same dreams and ambitions. We might not know what the future holds, however one thing is for certain, we know we want it together.

As we pulled up, I took in the scene. A small log cabin sat nestled amongst the trees, painted white wooden deck chairs encircled a fire pit and a picturesque lake lay beside it with a long slightly worn pier. It was as perfect as a painting and ours for the weekend.

I swung off my seatbelt and pushed open the door, making my way toward the cabin, I took two stairs at a time as I reached the wood framed stained-glass door. Grey followed at a much slower pace with the keys as I bounced from heel to heel, rubbing the palms of my hands together, waiting impatiently for him to open it. As we entered over the threshold, I took a quick glance around, not having much time to linger on my surroundings. Grey's hands found mine as he pulled me close and his lips met mine. We crashed into what I assumed was a side table, knocking a few ornaments over as our kisses grew more passionate. We finally made our way to an old tired taupe couch and fell clumsily side by side together. The inside of this place from what I could tell did not match the picture-perfect exterior. We laughed at our ungraceful landing and continued kissing, through our laughter. I broke away from him to really get a chance to examine where we were. Downstairs was an open plan layout with a kitchen resting to the back, behind a wooden staircase that's landing overlooked the entire downstairs. It wasn't a large cabin by any means, though it was obvious in its better kept days it would have been a perfect holiday home. The furniture was worn, and the TV still had a tape player. The kitchen was painted a duck egg blue, with laminate white countertops and a small island in the center, a few multi-colored mismatched bar stools tucked away underneath. As my eyes made their way back to Greyson, he smiled and leaned down to kiss me again. Before his lips could reach mine I pushed hard on his chest forcing him back and moving him away from me. 'Stop.' I said the words without even thinking and I didn't know why. Why did I just ask my boyfriend to stop kissing me? Greyson looked at me and parted his mouth about to speak, when a voice sounded from the open doorway.

'Rosie!'

Libby.

What was Libby doing here? Greyson jumped as soon as he heard her voice and we both stood up together to see not just Libby, but Caleb. What was *he* doing here? Isn't it enough that he doesn't approve of Greyson – but now he has to crash our weekend too? I looked at Greyson who wore a pinched expression, I tried to get him to look at me with no success.

'Caleb, Libby. What are you doing here?' Greyson frowned.

'We thought we would join you,' Caleb said, gritting his teeth and forcing a fake smile.

'Rosie, you knew we were joining you right?' Libby asked, as confusion washed over her features. She looked at Caleb expecting him to mirror her concerns.

'No,' I looked coldly at Caleb. Surely, he wouldn't go this far. Libby crossed her arms and glared at him.

'Well we're here now, so Grey, why don't you show me where our room is?' Caleb broke the awkward silence that had filled the room.

Greyson nodded and didn't look at me once before following Caleb outside to bring in our luggage.

'I'm sorry Rosie,' Libby genuinely looked apologetic as she walked toward me.

'It's ok, Caleb and I just have some things to work out and this is … unexpected,' I said, trying to snap out of my mood. Libby is one of those people that you just can't be angry around. It's one of her many qualities, she brings out the best in everyone.

'Well, let's leave the boys to the bags, there's a lake that looks like it's calling us. And then you're going to tell me what exactly you and Greyson were just arguing about.'

'I don't have my swimsuit Libby. It's buried in one of my bags.'

'So?' She shrugged as I kept pace beside her until we reached the edge of the lake.

'It's too late in the day, it'll be freezing.' I protested.

'Your clothes will keep you warm,' she paused, 'unless you would rather go help Greyson with your bags.' She smirked, as she tugged at the hair tie she kept around her wrist freeing it and pulling her hair into a high ponytail.

'Fine.' I looked down to the water, trying to guess how cold it would be against my skin.

'Three … Two … One.' Libby wrapped her hand around mine as she counted down and we leapt off the wooden pier into the icy cold water. The summer was rolling in and although the air held heat the water wasn't warm enough to swim in. I shivered at the initial impact of the water meeting my skin, I could feel the goosebumps prickle along every inch of my body. I moved my legs as fast as I could underneath the water, after a few movements my body acclimatized to the change in temperature.

'So, are you going to tell me what I walked in on back there?' Libby stood by her word and quizzed me not two seconds after we jumped into the lake, her lips chattering in the cold. She swam closer to me, giving me a knowing look. Libby, unlike Caleb, was fully supportive of my relationship with Greyson. She had even argued with Caleb about it, with no luck of course, that didn't matter, it mattered that she had tried.

'I'm not sure,' I answered sheepishly. It was probably obvious to Libby that I was embarrassed, she could usually tell just by looking at me how I was feeling. A perk that came from being friends since childhood.

'Well it looked pretty obvious to me, I've never seen him look so annoyed,' she tilted her head, an amused glint in her eyes.

'It's not funny Libs.' I looked away from her not wanting to meet her gaze.

Libby let out a loud almost overdramatic sigh, 'What happened?' This time the tone to her voice sounded different, it wasn't inquisitive as it had been before, it was empathetic.

'I really don't know. Everything was fine, better than fine, it was perfect and then I pushed him away and told him to stop kissing me. I don't know why or where it came from, it was like my body took over and I had no control over my own actions or the words that were escaping my mouth.' I tried explaining to her as best I could, but she obviously hadn't caught any of this by the shocked look on her face.

She tilted her head back into the water and looked toward the sky like she was being careful thinking up a response, then continued, 'It wasn't anything Caleb said to you was it? Because if it was, I swear I'm going to—'

'No Libs,' I interrupted her, 'it wasn't anything Caleb said.' That much I at least knew. Caleb might drive me crazy with his distaste toward my relationship but not enough to ever stop me being with Grey.

'Are you sure?'

'Promise,' I smiled. I just wish I knew why I suddenly didn't want to kiss my boyfriend.

We weren't in the water long before Greyson and Caleb joined us. I was grateful they arrived, and Libby would stop asking questions. Nerves grew in the pit of my stomach as I looked to Grey, I tried to think of an explanation for my actions, so far I was unable to come up with even one. As much as it annoyed me that Caleb and Libby had crashed our weekend, part of me was glad to have two other people here so I wouldn't have to be alone with Greyson now. For a moment while we floated in the water together it felt like it once was, with Libby, Caleb, Greyson and me. I knew I had to talk to Caleb about our fight, but that could wait until we got home. I also knew Greyson wouldn't let what happened earlier go so easily. As I lifted my head up, Greyson was watching me and gave a timid smile, I flicked up the water into his face giggling as he winced at the cold. We would be ok, I would come up with something to tell him when he would inevitably ask. I just wanted to enjoy this weekend, even if we had unspoken words between us and two unplanned guests.

Caleb and Libby lay the tinder down in the firepit, placing the kindling around it so each log met together in a slant. I lit the match, holding it to the tinder. The flames darted in a frantic swarm until reaching the kindling, the sparks from the fire crackled against the dark night, creating a warming glow. Libby popped open a bag of marshmallows piercing the end of each one with a stick, she walked two over to me and Greyson, before taking a seat on a deck chair across from us. Greyson wrapped a green tartan blanket across my shoulders, as the night air had cooled. I reached forward twisting the stick that held the marshmallow around in the flames. Hours passed while we made smores, laughed and reminisced around the now dying flames and it started to feel like it used to.

'More marshmallows,' Libby mumbled pointing toward the cabin. I was pretty sure she'd eaten half the bag by now, I was surprised she hadn't entered into a sugar induced coma.

'I've got it,' I replied, standing up and stretching, as the blanket that surrounded me fell back into my empty seat. I started to walk toward the cabin and got to the kitchen before I realised I was being followed, Caleb.

'We need to talk,' he said, peering across the kitchen island at me.

'Talk,' I replied coldly as I searched through the cupboards.

'Rosie, come on. This isn't us, we don't fight,' Caleb said sounding exhausted.

'As far as I'm concerned, you're the one with the problem. I can't remember telling you Libby isn't good enough for you.'

'You know that's not how I meant it.'

'Yeah well I'm not sure how else I'm meant to take it.'

'There's so much you don't understand, so much about Grey, you would understand more if you knew.'

'Know what Caleb?' Why was he being so vague and secretive?

'Just trust me, have I ever given you a reason not to?'

'Trust isn't the issue. The issue is you are telling me that you have a problem with my boyfriend. It's been a year, and it will be many more if I have a say, so you'd better get used to us being together pretty soon unless this is really how you want our relationship to be. I don't want things to be like this Cal. I love him and you need to respect that. He's your best friend. You should want him to be happy, you should want your sister to be happy and if that means us being together then you should accept that the way I have for you and Libby.'

'I'm sorry. I just, can't. I'm never going to be ok with you and him. We may be friends, but he knew how I felt about you both dating, he went behind my back and I can't forgive him for that. You're my sister Rosie, I'm always going to want what's best for you, and I know it isn't him. You're making a mistake. I don't want to fight about it anymore, you know where I stand on the subject and my mind isn't going to change. You can either hate me for it or we can forget this and move forward, just don't expect me to be supportive because I … I can't. You'll understand, someday.'

'I can't believe how petty you're being,' I slammed the cupboard door shut and narrowed my eyes at him.

'Rosie, please can we just move forward?' he begged.

'When you accept me and Greyson, then we can talk about moving forward, Caleb.'

'You know I'd do anything for you except that. I *can't*,' he reemphasized. He shifted his weight from foot to foot, he was nervous. A trait Caleb rarely, if ever displayed.

'Why, what's so awful about us being happy?' I crossed my arms tight across my chest and stared at him.

'Like I said, it's not just about happiness,' he looked down to his feet as if he were afraid to make eye contact with me.

'Then what is it about?' I ran my fingers through my hair and let out a slight groan in frustration.

'I can't tell you that,' his eyes met mine for a brief moment before looking away.

'What the hell do you mean you can't tell me?' I was shouting now, fed up with his vague replies, it was like he was trying to get me to read between the lines, which were impossible to understand.

'I don't want to fight anymore. I thought coming here this weekend would help clear the air between us,' he met my gaze now, his eyes pleading.

'Yes, you're right. Coming to my romantic weekend with my boyfriend that you have a problem with was going to clear up the air between us,' I rolled my eyes at him.

'I thought it might be good for us to hang out like old times. Then I saw you two together and I couldn't—' he paused and rested his hands on the island that was now a welcomed barrier between us.

'I know I'm your little sister Cal, but you don't have to protect me from my own boyfriend, I can make my own decisions.'

'But if you knew you wouldn't want him,' he sighed curling his fingers into his fists on the counter.

'Here you go again with being so vague, Caleb. What is it I don't know? Did he cheat on me or something?' I felt a tug in my chest at those words.

'No of course not, Grey's a good guy.'

'Ah-ha, you admit it,' I waved my finger at him, smiling for the first time since this conversation began.

'I never said he wasn't,' he sighed.

'Yet somehow even though he's a good guy he's just not right for me in your eyes, because he's your best friend.' I concluded.

'He's not my best friend.'

'Really, you're sinking that low now?'

'No, it's the truth,' he shrugged as if it were obvious.

'Then where is this best friend I haven't seen in the last three years? Should I be with him instead, what are you now, a matchmaker?' I teased.

'Can we just drop this and agree to disagree?' he looked over his shoulder as red rushed to his cheek. I looked at him curious, why did he just blush?

I wanted to stay mad at him, I really did, he is still my brother though and he has a tendency to be overprotective. He'll get over it someday, he'll have to accept Greyson. Then everything will go back to the way it was.

'Ok,' I let out a breath and replied in defeat.

He moved around the island, his arms stretched wide, pulling me into a hug, 'Thank you,' he whispered.

We walked out to the campfire together, the tension that had been there between us eased. Even though we hadn't resolved everything yet, actually that's a lie, we had literally run around in circles and resolved nothing. Caleb just had a way of winning me over, and I honestly wished I could stand my ground a little longer with him. We continued eating, laughing and sharing stories until the sun started to rise and the flames had completely died out, that was our cue to go to bed. We walked into the cabin as I went to the bedroom door that rested just off the living room. I was expecting to see Greyson's bag there beside mine, but instead I was greeted with Libby's many bags instead.

'Sorry Libby, I must have walked into the wrong room,' I started to leave.

'Don't tell me you didn't know,' she said seeming annoyed.

'What?' I sighed in frustration.

'We are sharing a room, Caleb told me you wanted to

share with me, and by the look on your face you had no idea. I'll go talk to him—'

'No, it's ok,' I interrupted Libby for the second time today. Caleb had better thank me later because I have managed to save him from her wrath on two occasions, even though he doesn't deserve it.

'You sure?' she asked.

'Yep,' I replied forcing a smile. Although I wanted to share a room with Greyson, I didn't want him asking me about earlier. So, I decided to avoid him and keep the room arrangement my brother had so kindly adjusted for me. I also didn't have the energy to fight with Caleb again tonight, he really has no limits. I sighed and collapsed on the bed. It was old, lumpy and creaked every time I moved, great. I guess it was never going to be a romantic weekend away anyway, they really should update their website; it was a lot more run down than we were expecting.

The next morning, I woke early, really early so I would escape seeing Caleb and giving him another piece of my mind for last night's bedroom fiasco. I decided to take a walk through the forest trail and admire the view of the lake. The interior of the cabin may have been undesirable but the natural beauty that surrounded it made braving getting some rare disease from inside worth it. It wasn't long until I was joined by a very welcomed guest.

'Hey sweetheart,' he exhaled, catching his breath as he ran to catch up with me.

'Sorry about all this, I had no idea Caleb and Libby planned on coming, not that I mind, I just thought it would be you and me. You know?' he gave me an apologetic glance.

'It's ok, I should be the one apologizing; he is my brother after all.'

He smiled, then hesitated before leaning down to place a kiss on my lips, it wasn't the passionate kisses we had shared the day before, though it was enough to leave me wanting more. Why did I tell him to stop yesterday? Honestly, sometimes I think there really is something wrong with me.

'So—' Greyson started. 'Can I ask what happened yesterday?' He stuttered on his words, his eyes searching mine for an explanation, one I didn't possess. The best

I could come up with was that I'm an idiot. Although no doubt that isn't what he is looking for from me. Why do I always have to overcomplicate everything?

'I … I don't know. I'm sorry.'

'Don't apologize. Honestly Rosie, I … I just—' he stopped as he fidgeted with the pockets of his jeans, his eyes focused on the ground.

'What?' I pushed.

'I thought it was something I did, and I wanted to apologize to you in case I did something wrong.'

'No. You did nothing wrong. I have no idea what happened, I'm sorry Grey, I really am. Please don't think you ever did something wrong, ok?

His body relaxed, as he leaned his head down, his mouth touching mine, gentle at first as if it were a test, to see if I'd push him away again. My emotions felt nothing like they had yesterday, the last thing I wanted to do was push Greyson away. I pulled on his jacket moving his body closer to mine, and he deepened our kiss.

By the time we got back to the cabin, Caleb and Libby were awake and cooking breakfast. Caleb wore his white oversized hoodie from last night and yawned as he held one arm around Libby, while she flipped a pancake into the air. Her auburn hair French braided into pig tails, rested against the same white t-shirt that peaked out from under the black denim dungarees she wore last night. They hadn't even noticed Grey and I until we reached the island, the screeching of the stools scraped along the tiled flooring as we took a seat. Libby added the pancakes to the already stacked plate in front of us, setting the frying pan back into the sink.

'Eat up.' She looked to me and then Grey and smirked. We could have entire conversations with one look, the unspoken words danced between us, the boys oblivious to our conversation.

Once we finished up our breakfast, I helped Libby with the dishes. I made my way into our room fishing out my red swimsuit that of course was at the very bottom of the last bag I checked. I slipped it on, grabbing a light grey zip up hoodie and some trainers before running upstairs to Greys room so I could ask him to go to the lake with me. I was hoping we could get some more alone time together before we leave tomorrow. I approached his room and reached for the door handle about to push the door open, when I heard two loud angry voices.

'Caleb, stop. You know I love her.'

'She's my sister man, you couldn't date any other girl? What about that girl, what was her name … oh yeah Erin? She was all over you at that party.'

'And I told her I wasn't interested because I'm with Rosie.'

'Yeah but what I'm saying is if you weren't with Rosie you could easily have your pick of the girls.'

'Caleb, stop. I've really had enough of this. Every party we go to when she's not there you're sending girls to me telling them I'm available. I love her, just let it go.'

'Yeah well it didn't seem like it yesterday.'

'That's between me and Rosie.'

'Well I'm just saying it looked like you two aren't doing so well together.'

'Stay out of it Caleb.'

'Won't you just consider what I've said?'

'NO!'

I heard heavy footsteps approaching the door, most likely Greyson, and I had nowhere to go. Damn it, now they would know I had been listening. I tried pacing back a few steps, so it looked like I was just walking down the hallway and not standing with my ear pressed up against the door, getting angrier and angrier at Caleb; this was just a vicious cycle now.

The door opened and out walked Greyson, shirtless in his shorts and ready for the lake – he must have read my mind. His eyes widened when he saw me, looking surprised that I was standing there and probably a little concerned that I had just heard his argument with Caleb. Then his gaze drifted to my body and my outfit, it was a simple red swimsuit I had bought just over a year ago at Libby's insistence, for a hot tub party that Libby hosted, and when I say party, I mean me, Caleb, Grey and Libby's inflatable hot tub.

'You look beautiful Rosie,' he grinned.

I smiled, feeling a lot more confident. I'm not sure why, it's not like he's never seen me in a swimsuit before. In fact, he's seen me in this exact one, but not since he's been my boyfriend.

I pulled on the zip of my jacket tugging it up, 'I was just coming to see if you wanted to come down to the lake with me,' I gestured for us to leave.

We picked a spot down by the lake far away from Libby and Caleb. I was sorry I couldn't spend time with Libby but right now Caleb wasn't doing much to be liked. Even though we did have our 'clearing the air' conversation last night, he still wouldn't let it go if what I heard in the hallway had anything to do with it, and don't even get me started on the passing girls Grey's way thing either. I'm going to kill him.

We lay down on a small day bed, that sat by the edge of the lake. I rested my head on his chest as he let out a deep sigh, running his hand gently up and down the curves of my waist.

'What was that about?' I asked.

'You heard that,' he sighed.

'Not everything, but enough.'

'I don't think he's ever going to be ok with us, I think we're going to have to be ok with the fact we aren't going to get his approval. I mean, maybe when we're forty he'll let it go,' he smirked.

'I don't know, Caleb can hold a grudge,' we both stared at each other before breaking into laughter.

That would be some long grudge even for Cal to hold onto, if anyone could do it though, it would be him. Then the words Greyson just spoke entered my mind, 'when we're forty.' I smiled a big cheesy smile, he noticed shaking his head and smirking back at me. I rested my chin on his chest grinning up at him, my shoulders still shaking with laughter.

'So … does Caleb really send girls to you at parties? I played with the tips of his fingers stroking them with mine.

Greyson started to laugh again until he looked down to see my face and stopped. I wasn't stupid enough to think that girls wouldn't find him attractive. I mean seriously, you just have to look at him to know girls would be lining up for him and I remembered that from when we were just friends. The thought of Caleb purposefully ushering girls in his direction to tempt him hit a nerve.

'Hey,' he pulled my chin up gently with his hand so that I was looking into his eyes.

'None of those girls even came close to you. I love *you*.'

He had this effect over me that could calm me in an instant. A word, a touch, that's all it would take and suddenly, like a flame to ice, all my insecurities melted away until they became nothing. We fell asleep together on that little day bed and it felt so peaceful that I wished we could have stayed there forever.

Chapter 3

'Table four, orders up.'

I sighed, carefully lifting and balancing the hot plates and walked toward table four. Working at Sleepy Thistle was not ideal. It felt like everyone else had everything together, already working on their futures and here I was in the same job for the past three years. I had debated with the idea of returning to university and completing another degree, but I had the same problem. I still had no idea what I wanted to do for a career. I always figured it would just appear before me someday and I would just know, I'm still waiting. But my time's ran out and upon returning from the cabin yesterday, I had told my dad I would take the job. Did I instantly regret it? Yes. I knew though if I wanted to start making real money and saving for a place to eventually move into with Grey then I had to grow up and swallow my pride. I've been doing this job that I hate for the last three years, what's another fifty plus in another job I hate? I was going to have to revisit that whole back to university idea.

'Here you go, can I get you anything else?' I attentively set the plates in front of an elderly couple that were deep in conversation with one another.

'No thank you dear,' the old lady gave me a friendly smile, before making a start on her meal and continuing with her conversation.

As I walked back toward the counter, I glanced up at the clock that hung on the exposed brick wall, it was now eleven in the morning, a small smile made its way to my lips. One of the benefits of this job was that it was right beside Greyson's work, which meant we got to spend our break and lunches together, that was a perk I would definitely miss in my new job.

'Kane, I'm taking my break now,' I shouted into the back so my boss could hear me.

I removed my black apron and set it beneath the countertop. Kane was the best boss anyone could ask for he was only a year older than Greyson. And his parents had gifted him the restaurant so they could retire early, giving him a business and a job. He was covered head to toe in tattoos, everywhere apart from his face. He takes pride in showing them off, each one holds a story or a meaning behind it. I don't even know how you have that many tattoos with stories and meaning but that's Kane. His long dark hair is always tied back into a bun, his leather biker jacket, that I'm convinced I've never seen him without hangs proudly around his shoulders. How he wears that in a stuffy restaurant without dying of heat exhaustion I will never know. He would look intimidating if you didn't know him, but I've worked here for three years, and we've actually become really good friends. He hates working at the restaurant too and is always talking about his idea to renovate it into a club for his band. Unfortunately, the only rule his parents made was that the restaurant was to stay in the exact same condition whilst in the family name. I guess they aren't the most supportive of his ambitions. We come up with new ideas every day it feels like, to try and make his dreams a reality so far, our best idea of 'rock restaurant' didn't enthuse his parents like it did us, still we can try right?

I walked across the gravel and took a seat at a small light wooden picnic table situated at the back of the restaurant, it was our lunch break area with one table, a bin and a shelter for smokers.

'Hey,' Greyson leaned in and kissed my cheek. 'How's work going?'

I rolled my eyes.

'That bad?' he said frowning, he sat down next to me pulling out a protein bar from his pocket and began to unwrap it.

'Let's not talk about work, let's talk about tonight,' I changed the subject, and took a bite out of my apple.

'About tonight, I can't go,' he stopped eating and looked at me, a guilty expression covered his features.

'Grey you've been looking forward to this for weeks, what happened?'

'They changed the rota last minute after Hunter called in sick,' he said sighing.

'Is there no way you can get out of it?' I asked hopeful, even though I already knew if there was any way Grey could have avoided it, he would have.

'I'm really sorry. I know we've planned on this for a

while, but my boss needs me to cover him tonight. I won't be out until eight and that doesn't leave enough time for the three-hour trip to Glasgow.'

'It's ok, I'll ask Libby to go with me instead,' I smiled so he wouldn't see my disappointment.

'Thanks sweetheart,' he said, leaning in to kiss me.

I changed the subject after that and asked Grey about his day. He worked in the bank next door to the restaurant and, unlike me he enjoyed his job. He filled me in on some of the office antics and talked to me about our plans for the weekend. We had been sitting there lost in conversation when it suddenly dawned on me.

'What time is it?'

'Eleven fifteen, you're late again aren't you?' he chuckled.

'I'll text you later Grey, got to go,' I said, rushing to my feet. As I ran quickly into the restaurant, Kane gave me a stern look and then smiled at me shaking his head.

'Still having trouble with time Rosie?' Kane grinned. Time keeping definitely wasn't a strength of mine.

'Sorry Kane.'

'I came up with another one,' he said with excitement in his voice.

'Well go on then, share with the class,' I said swinging

my apron over my head so I could start helping him with the approaching lunch time rush.

'Order's up,' Parker shouted from the kitchen.

'Hold that thought Kane, let me get this to table nine,' I walked over to a very pale, tall, middle aged man with piercing black eyes. Are black eyes a thing? Well this guy either had some crazy contacts or they were the creepiest eyes I've ever seen.

'Here's your order sir, can I get you anything else?' I swallowed, suddenly feeling nervous in his presence.

He looked me up and down, licking his lips and I felt the hairs on the back of my neck stand up, this guy was bad news.

'No …' he paused, glancing at my name tag, 'Rosie. That'll be all.'

I shuddered a little at the sound of my name passing his lips. I rushed back to the counter still a little creeped out by the grim reaper at table nine, but I shrugged it off; we've seen our fair share of strange people in this town.

'Ok, so let's hear it Kane.'

'You sure you are ready? Cos this one, it's gonna be the winner,' he said, confident.

'YES,' Parker and I shouted at the same time. Parker

was in Kane's band but knew how to work a fryer, so Kane hired him. He was dressed in a similar fashion to Kane, sans leather jacket; the kitchen was definitely too hot for that.

'Ok, three words, "open mic restaurant", he moved his hands like he was showing us his vision.

'That's the exact same thing as rocker restaurant,' I said smiling and shaking my head.

'No, it's not. It's completely different,' Kane said defensively.

'Rosie is right man, it's the same thing, it's never going to fly with the parents.'

Kane let out a sigh, 'You two just don't get creative genius when you see it.'

Parker, Kane and I burst into a fit of laughter. I felt bad for him, he really just wanted to turn this place into something this small town was missing, unfortunately it looked like Sleepy Thistle would be around for a while.

Although we were busy, work seemed to go so slowly. I waited as each hour passed for my shift to be over and once the clock struck six, I was out of there in a flash. I rushed to my car and threw my handbag into the back seat, I pulled down to open my glove compartment revealing two concert tickets. Hopefully Libby would be able to go in Grey's place. I dialed Libby's number, waiting patiently for her to answer. Nothing. Great. It was a three-hour drive and I really wanted the company. I sighed and tilted my head back when I caught sight of Kane in my rear-view mirror, I stuffed the tickets into my pocket, swung open the car door and ran over to him.

'Kane,' I yelled, slightly out of breath from my unnecessary sprint.

He stopped in his tracks and frowned at me, 'What is it Rosie?' he tilted his head as if assessing me.

'Are you working the evening shift tonight?' my voice hitched between breaths.

'No.' he paused as he reached into his jacket pulling out a pre-rolled cigarette and lighter, holding the cigarette between his lips and giving me a curious look as he lit it. 'Why?' he continued.

'What are you doing tonight?'

He raised his eyebrow probably wondering where this was going. I reached into my pocket and pulled out the two concert tickets. It was a small band Greyson and I had seen on one of our first dates. He got me the tickets for my birthday a while ago. It was probably not Kane's scene at all, but it was him or Caleb and I didn't fancy the 'Why are you trying to get my boyfriend to go out with other girls?' argument with him tonight. I handed Kane the tickets.

'Want to go to a concert?' I smiled at him, hoping he'd say yes.

He flicked the tickets around in his hand reading the name of the band. He shook his head and smiled, 'sure, beats avoiding my parents knocking down my new restaurant idea, again.'

He walked toward my car still smoking and I looked at him, then the cigarette, and raised my eyebrow.

'Come on Rosie, your car is like a hundred years old,' he joked.

'I'll have you know it's a 2009 model,' I opened my mouth wide, pretending to be shocked and held my hand to my heart feigning hurt.

He chuckled and pleaded, 'What if I roll the window down?'

'Ok,' I conceded with a loud overexaggerated sigh.

I started the engine and pulled out of the car park, taking a right onto the motorway to begin our journey, everything always seemed so far away from our town.

'So how come you had a spare ticket last minute?' Kane asked, curious.

'Greyson had to cover for a guy that called in sick,' I said with a shrug.

'Office work, so exciting, all those numbers aren't going to balance themselves,' he replied sarcastically.

'I know it's going to kill me,' I shook my head.

'You know your job is always open at the restaurant,' Kane said reassuring me.

He had reminded me of this several times since I had told him this morning. He knew all too well the pressures that parents could use to manipulate decisions. Although my situation was different to Kane's, I knew that no matter what I decided my dad would support me, even if he didn't agree, he at least had good intentions. The same unfortunately couldn't be said about Kane's parents. On the few occasions I had met them they had managed to leave a lasting impression, and not a good one.

'Thanks Kane, but as much as I hate to say it my dad's right, I need something that pays a bit more so me and Grey can eventually move out.'

'So, you and Greyson are end game then?' He took a final drag of his cigarette and threw it out of the open window.

I had a habit of smiling anytime anyone mentioned Greyson and I being in this for the long haul. I couldn't help but get all giddy like I'd won the best prize at the fair.

'Yeah I hope so', I smirked.

He smiled at me knowingly.

'He's a lucky guy. If he has any sense at all he'll never let you go.'

Kane wasn't usually sentimental like that but now and again he would just throw a sentence out and be sweet. He's especially this way at the moment because his girlfriend Molly just broke up with him. He's been roaming about like Gatsby ever since. If he wasn't so heartbroken it would have been a little funny.

'I'm gonna stay over at a friend's house; it's close by the concert so if you want to crash there for the night, you're more than welcome?' he asked, looking up from his phone and waiting before he finished his text.

'Thanks, but I want to get home. It's my day off tomorrow and my dad wanted me to go into his office for an introduction. I'll be replacing you and Parker with my dad and Caleb soon.'

'Good luck with that, I think I'd rather die than work with my family,' he laughed.

The hours passed by quickly enough, it would have been even faster if Greyson were here, but it wasn't his fault. Kane and I talked and discussed in detail how he would get this new idea past his parents. We listened to a CD he gave me a few months ago of his band, he told me the story behind each of the songs, skipping by one titled 'Molly.'

The concert was good even Kane seemed to enjoy it. After the last song had finished, he walked me out to my car and made sure I'd be ok to drive home; it was already past two in the morning, I insisted I was fine, I really did feel ok. I planned on stopping by a drive thru and getting some coffee just in case though, with that we said our goodbyes. I would see him on Wednesday for my next shift, where I'm sure I'll hear all about how his parents turned down yet another genius idea. He told me to text him when I arrived home safe and waved me off. I pulled up to the drive thru and placed my order, I decided to pull over before hitting the motorway to text Grey and Caleb; they would only worry otherwise. Sure enough, I had four messages in my inbox, one from Greyson, two from Caleb and one from Libby. I took a sip of my coffee and opened up the first text.

Libby: Hey sorry I missed your call everything ok?

I decided to leave texting Libby back until tomorrow; there was no point waking her to tell her I went to a concert.

Caleb: Rosie, you didn't come home, where are you? Are you with Greyson?

Caleb: Please text me back it's getting late and you still aren't home?

Greyson: Hey sweetheart, did Libby end up going with you?

I replied first to Greyson.

Rosie: No Kane did but he's staying with a friend tonight so I'm making the drive back by myself. I'll text you when I get home.

He replied almost straight away.

Greyson: Ok drive safe, pull over and call me if you get too tired, I'll come get you.

I typed in Caleb's name to reply to him next.

Rosie: All good just went to a concert, on the drive up now will be home in a few hours. Don't wait up.

He replied straight away. I knew he wouldn't sleep until he knew I was ok. That's Caleb being overprotective again.

Caleb: Just be careful Rosie. Text me if you need me. I need to talk to you tomorrow, it's important.

Chapter 4

I tried to keep myself awake by rolling down the window and blasting the radio as loud as it could go, but it wasn't working; my eyes were closing. I put my foot on the accelerator and pushed it to the floor. *I just need to get home*. The roads were covered with water, and rain cascaded down thudding against the windscreen. The sound was almost louder than the radio, and my wipers were frantically trying to clear it away. An animal darted from the side of the road, I swerved and hit my brakes hard, too hard. My car span out of control, crashing through the barrier and landing in the river underneath.

I lost consciousness for minutes. When I opened my

eyes again, I could see the water pouring in rapidly. I tried to force the door open, nothing. I tried to smash the window, nothing. The water was rising quickly, reaching up to my shoulders. I knew it would only be a matter of time before I had to hold my breath, so I started to prepare myself. Taking in as many deep breaths as possible, I focused on the feeling of the air entering my lungs as if it would be the last time I would ever experience the sensation. I couldn't think about anything else, I wouldn't allow myself to. I needed to survive, to find a way out. There had to be another way, another window to try and break open. Something. Anything. I couldn't let go of the glimmer of hope that was still lingering in my mind.

I took a deep breath as the water covered my chin, this *was* it. I tried unbuckling my seat belt, hoping I could swim into the back of the car to explore other options, but it wouldn't budge. I took one last deep breath before my entire body was underwater. I knew I had to keep calm because if I struggled, I wouldn't be able to hold my breath much longer. Then, after what felt like seconds, I let the first rush of water in and panicked. I felt a tearing and burning sensation in my chest as it entered my lungs, the pain unbearable.

I thought about everything I hadn't done yet, everything I was so afraid to do. I thought about my family and Greyson and how I would never see their faces again. Memories danced in my mind almost taunting me. I let the water in once more as the first breath caused me to choke and inhale again but this time it didn't hurt as much. After a couple more breaths it had stopped hurting, and I relaxed, drifting slowly into unconsciousness.

Chapter 5

'I think she's waking up now, I'll call you back.'

I opened my eyes to see a man standing across the room, talking on what looked like a phone. My focus wasn't perfect yet so I couldn't make out his features. I blinked a few times and rubbed my eyes, glancing back to where the man was standing, he was in focus now. He looked young, older than me though, probably around Grey's age. He was tall, muscular with short disheveled dark hair and slightly tanned skin. I looked around trying to gather where exactly I was. Although it just looked like an empty warehouse, the bed I was lying on was oddly centered in the room, a long table stretched along the far right side and three very large windows reached to the ceiling on the far left, though all I was able to see through them was darkness, indicating it was still night. I couldn't see behind me but in front of me there was a small door, which I assumed would be the exit, my escape. I groaned as I attempted to sit up, feeling a sudden sharp pain in my throat and the man rushed over from where he had previously been standing.

'Where am I?' I asked, my throat felt as if it were burning, and I instinctively lifted my hand to grasp it.

'You're safe,' he said giving me a reassuring smile.

Now he was closer I could fully make out the rest of his features. He had the bluest eyes I think I've ever seen. His eyelashes were long enough to graze the skin beneath his eyes, and his messy black hair was swept to the right side of his forehead. His features were masculine and defined. He had a long silver scar trailing down his right cheek and another traced the left side of his neck, the scars did nothing but add to his attractiveness. He was without a doubt an extremely handsome man. Looking at him, I felt like I knew him somehow. His expression was kind and empathetic making me feel at ease in his presence.

'What happened to me?'

'Where am I?'

'Why am I not in hospital?'

I spoke as if I couldn't get the words out fast enough, I needed answers and I needed them now. Each word that I spoke sounded hoarser than the last, though the pain started to ease.

He smiled shaking his head. 'One question at a time.' He said then continued, 'You were in a car accident, your car went into the river, I jumped in after you.' My memory flashed back to the water and I shuttered. He looked at me and then continued to answer my many questions.

'I took you here so I could make sure you were ok before we reported back to Kai. This is the safest place for you, it's not like the humans could help you anyway,' he started laughing and looked at me to follow, like it was a joke I would understand.

He's insane, what exactly did he mean by "the humans?" I felt the colour drain from my face as I realised just how much trouble I was in.

Then for some strange, probably equally insane reason, I felt myself drawn to him. I found myself wanting to know what he meant and who exactly he thought I was. I still didn't see him as a threat, even though everything in my head told me to run. I couldn't fight the overwhelming urge to stay and let him finish. He was talking to me like he had known me for years. I took a deep breath and asked him another question, hoping I had made the right decision.

'What exactly do you mean by humans?'

He seemed taken aback by my question and his expression turned serious.

'*They* really did it. All this time I thought—' he stopped abruptly, looking down to the ground as if choosing his words carefully, then looked back into my eyes and continued.

'You don't even know who I am do you?'

I shook my head, tensing my eyebrows empathetically, suddenly feeling intense sadness, knowing my answer was hurting him.

'I'm sorry,' he exhaled.

'I'm sure you probably think I've lost my mind. I didn't mean to overwhelm you. I just thought … I thought you would remember me if you saw me Rosie.'

I could feel my heart pounding against my chest. How did he know my name?

'I guess I'm going to have to get your memory back the

hard way,' he looked at me apologetically.

'Wha … What do you mean the hard way?' I shuddered at what he might mean by those words.

'How do you know my name?' I demanded.

'I guess I will start with the basics, my name is Ezra,' he sighed.

'You have known me your whole life Rosie. Well, almost eighteen years of it to be exact. You won't remember this because *they* took your memories from you and sent you here to Earth to protect you,' he looked at me studying my face, and sighed again.

'I need you to get your memories back, we need you to join us. I wish I didn't have to do this to you, I had hoped when you saw me it would all come back to you, but they really took everything from you.' He rubbed at the top of his forehead.

I looked at him with confusion, shock and possibly horror too. I decided it was time to bargain with him. I needed to get home to my family and get as far away from this man as possible.

'Look, Ezra. I don't know how you know my name, who you are or what it is that you want from me, but I can tell you that if you don't let me go now, I'll have no choice but to call the police. I have family that will be looking for me right now.' I spoke clearly and emphasized the last line, letting him know it would be noticed if I went missing, and he wouldn't get away with whatever plan he had.

He looked at me with a grin and his eyes narrowed. He turned around slowly, walking toward the table that stretched across the right side of the warehouse. It was as if he didn't take heed of my words, like they meant nothing to him.

I took this opportunity while he seemed distracted to make a run for it. I eyed the door facing me and hoped I would reach it in time. As I stood, I felt my legs wobble and buckle beneath me, before I could even hit the ground I was in his arms.

'Careful, you've just been in a car accident. You need to take it slow.'

He laid me back down on the bed gently, clearly not realising my plan was to escape. I watched as he reached into his pocket and pulled out what looked like a needle. I felt my body start to tremble.

He leaned in close to me and said softly, 'It will all make sense soon Rosie, I promise.'

His gentle tone didn't do much to comfort me, I had seen stories like this on the news. He was going to kill me. I wanted to scream and fight, instead I just laid there frozen staring at the large needle in his hand. He took the cap off the top of the needle and injected a blue substance into my left arm. I winced at the sudden sharp pain, feeling helpless. I lost consciousness immediately and drifted into a dreamlike trance.

I saw everything. It felt like a dream only somehow, I knew it wasn't, I *knew* it was real. My parents, my older brother Caleb, even Libby. Everything was a lie. Ezra was right. I was from a different world, Atheria.

My parents, my real parents, Solon and Imelda, were leaders in our world and fought back against a rebellion that threatened to destroy Atheria. When things became dangerous, they sent me to Earth and erased my memories of everyone and everything that had been in my life before, replacing them with new memories of a human life. Memories taken from other humans and merged together to create a believable lie.

They'd formed memories in my mind and in those around me, to make them and I believe that I had been in their lives all along. I saw how much they believed in their cause and they were willing to sacrifice everything for it, including me.

Ezra had been my childhood best friend and later my boyfriend, before they sent me away. We shared such an unbreakable bond. He came to see me the night before I left, he was meant to be leaving a day after me and promised that he would find me no matter what. He kept his word, like he always has, though we both had no idea they would take my memories.

I could feel all of my emotions now, like opening a wound. It was unbearable. I felt so much love for Ezra and my parents, yet so much sadness that my memories of my human childhood and life were just an illusion. I suddenly felt as if a void had opened up beneath me and swallowed everything I thought I once knew. Things that were so real to me, that were so important to me. Gone. I saw it all in flashes as if it were a film, all the memories that were taken were replaced with stolen memories from someone else's life.

The time I cut my knee open when I was just ten years old and Caleb had ripped the bottom of his shirt to stop the bleeding, he had carried me the whole way home that day.

The day our family dog Stella died, Caleb had stayed in my room and comforted me until I fell asleep. It was just a lie, someone else's life. Not mine. The forged memories stayed stagnant in my mind, as my real memories took their place. Though I still remembered everything I once thought to be true from my human life, I could now tell which of my memories were mine and which had been altered. My real, old memories filled my mind, memories of my mother and father, my home and Ezra. I had lost so much in a moment, yet I gained so much in return, because I gained them. It only left two people that remained real from my human life, Libby and Greyson. Everything with Grey was still real, and with Libby, our childhood together had been fabricated but the last three years had been real.

I opened my eyes, feeling Ezra holding my hand in his and stroking it gently. 'I was wondering when you'd wake up.' I looked down to our hands together, noticing the same silver scarring that trailed along his neck and cheek branching off up his arm too many for me to count.

'What happened to you?' I asked my eyes still focused on his skin. For whatever reason he didn't arrive a day after me that much I knew.

'We can talk about that another time.' he leaned in

wrapping his arms around me, surrounding me in his warmth that I had longed for without knowing. Tears stung in my eyes before escaping, he stroked the back of my hair with his hand as I let out every shred of emotion that was buried inside.

'It will be ok. I know it's a lot to take in at once, but I promise we'll figure it out, like we always do,' he assured me.

He placed my head in his hands, using his thumb to brush away my tears. Pulling me close again he kissed my forehead softly, lowering his voice to a whisper he spoke, 'I've waited so long for this moment, to have you back in my arms.'

I knew I needed to tell him about Greyson and I needed him to tell me the parts I never got the chance to know. Where are my parents? What did they know back then that they needed to protect me from so desperately? What had happened to him? I needed Ezra to answer my questions, though first I just wanted to enjoy having him with me once more. It was such a strange feeling, missing someone so much yet not having thought about them one day for three years. I breathed in his familiar scent and embraced every second of his arms around me. It was like I had subconsciously been waiting for this moment too without even realising it.

We curled up together on the large bed, Ezra holding me while I continued to ask questions. His hands were placed on my waist, moving slowly up and down, comforting me. His touch sent a shiver down my spine, I missed him. Why did everything have to be so complicated now?

'I think we need to get some sleep before we meet Kai in the morning,' he whispered.

'I think you're right but, I still don't know who Kai is.'

He started to laugh. I had forgotten how much I loved his laugh.

'Don't worry, you never met Kai, he's our new leader. He took over after our parents—' he looked concerned, like he didn't want to continue in case it upset me.

'What? What is it? you can tell me Ezra.'

'After our parents died,' he exhaled his eyes settled in on mine.

The words stung me. My parents were dead. Tears welled in my eyes and began to fall, 'How?' I stuttered.

He glanced down, gathering his thoughts carefully choosing his words. 'I think you've taken in quite a lot of information today already, maybe we should save the rest for tomorrow?'

I nodded trusting him as he pulled me back into his arms wiping away my tears. I wanted to know what had happened to them and I wasn't going to let it go. They had died, and based on what Ezra had told me, it wasn't through natural causes. Someone had done this. I felt a sting of pain rush through my body, the feeling was almost too much to bear. My parents were dead. I repeated it over and over in my mind, though those words never quite stuck. It felt cruel, everything I had learned today. My human parents weren't even my parents, Caleb wasn't my brother, Libby's friendship had been built on a lie, Ezra didn't know about Greyson yet and Greyson didn't know about Ezra, and I feared that when they inevitably found out about each other I would lose them both, and then the worst of all of it my parents were dead. I wept into Ezra's chest for what felt like hours, the tears never seeming to slow down. He held me there in a silence that was peaceful. I had never lost anyone apart from my grandparents when I was younger, and that loss felt very different to this loss. That was natural, a fact of life, but this, this was stolen from me.

I stopped crying, not because I wanted to, but because my body couldn't anymore. I felt numb, I wanted so badly to hear my mother's voice again and my father's loud echoing laughter that had filled our home with so much joy. For a brief moment I wished Ezra hadn't given me my memories back, but I shook that thought away. I turned my body away from his, looking toward the windows. I could see the night sky was beginning to lighten, I closed my eyes hoping to sleep. To wake up back home, in my real home with my family surrounding me and this, nothing more than a nightmare.

Ezra seemed to drift to sleep immediately, as tired as I was, I couldn't stop thinking about the day and about every drop of knowledge I now held. I allowed my mind to drift from my parents to the questions that still remained, like how I was going to face my human parents, Libby, Caleb and most importantly, Greyson. I felt a pang of guilt when I thought about him. Here I was lying sleeping next to another man, a man I had loved, that I still love, while Greyson was probably worried sick about me. How was I going to explain this to him? To think I had thought my life was complicated, choosing a career after university, now I had two worlds to choose between.

Chapter 6

I slowly opened my eyes and looked up to the ceiling, I guess this *was* real. It didn't take long before the pain from yesterday flashed back to me, my eyes felt red and puffy from all the tears that I had shed. I stood up and decided to look for Ezra who was no longer lying beside me. As I had discovered last night there wasn't much in the warehouse, the three large windows were now letting in light, that caused me to squint slightly. My gaze drifted to my right and toward the long table when I noticed a few objects scattered across it. I walked over to take a closer look. I came to a small bright red book with the initials AE inscribed in beautiful gold writing. I ran my fingers over the inscription and contemplated opening it for a moment, though I hesitated when I realised those initials would have likely been Ezra's parents, Amelia and Elias. Beside it lay the needle and the vial of what had been the blue serum that Ezra had given me to return my memories. I shuddered at the thought of the previous night and all I had learnt, the sadness overwhelmed me again and my thoughts drifted to my parents.

I continued my search for Ezra and pulled the unusually small warehouse door open, letting in more of the sunlight. A soft breeze blew my hair and I reached up to tuck a few strands behind my ears. I could see now that the warehouse we had stayed in last night was nestled amongst the forest. Light beamed through the treetops and cascaded down on a small lake that rippled softly against the wind, only a few feet away from where I stood. The exact location was still a mystery to me. As my gaze drifted over the lake and the morning sun glistened on the water my eyes met his. He had decided to go for a morning swim and his clothes lay on a small wooden bench beside the water.

I took a step toward him when I felt a sudden buzzing from my pocket. I reached in and pulled out my phone. How is it *still* working? Missed calls from my parents,

Caleb, Greyson and Libby. I needed to talk to them, I owed them that at least. My childhood may have been an illusion but the last three years, that *was* real. They were probably really worried at this stage; I'd now been gone for a few days. What if they found my car in the river? They would assume the worst. I needed to come up with some sort of an explanation for my disappearance. I tried to swipe my phone open to text them back, but it had frozen, I guess it was damaged after all.

Ezra had now started to make his way out of the water, I turned around to give him some privacy to change. It took him merely seconds before he was by my side. His hair was still wet as he looked down at the phone nestled in my hand, buzzing with incoming phone calls and messages that I couldn't answer.

'How are you?' Ezra asked, his eyes piercing into mine.

'I've been better,' I tried to joke but by his reaction he could see straight through me. I was a mess. My red blotchy features probably gave that away. My exterior only showed half of what was going on inside my head though. The grief I felt for my parents came in waves, I didn't know that when you lost someone so precious you could feel not just emotional pain but physical. It hurt that they were now gone, and grief was something I now knew I didn't care for. Ezra moved closer to me, his blue eyes looked even brighter in the light of the day and I had forgotten how much I loved those eyes. For a moment looking at him, the loss I felt got lighter. We still had each other. My phone buzzed again, pulling me back to reality. I exhaled, looking down at the messages I couldn't answer.

'You still care about them, don't you?' he sighed and gestured to my phone.

'I need to go back, I can't just leave them thinking the worst,' I tucked my phone back inside my pocket.

He looked at me, surprisingly with an excited expression, took a deep breath and said, 'Ok, I'll take you back and I'll explain everything to them. But you have to come and meet Kai first … deal?' He grinned smugly, like he was proud of himself.

'Blackmailing me now, are you?' I said, narrowing my eyes and smiling at him, he shrugged as his lip tugged upwards into a smirk.

'Ok. But Ezra, one more thing, I need to tell you something first,' I paused for a second, knowing this probably wasn't the ideal moment to tell him about Greyson, but he was going to find out when we reached the house and I didn't have a whole lot of time left.

'I have a … a … *boyfriend*,' I swallowed hard, stuttering on my words, and as I examined his face my heart dropped.

'Boyfriend?' he spoke so quietly I could barely hear him.

'I didn't know about you, about us,' I rushed the words out as quickly as I could, trying my best to explain myself. I wanted to take it back, to take it all back, but I knew I had to tell him about Greyson. I owed that to both of them, even if I had conflicting feelings for Ezra now. I didn't want to hurt him, though I knew that look on his face and it was too late, my words had already opened a wound. I never thought I would ever hurt Ezra and I felt terrible that I had managed to cause him more unnecessary pain.

'We don't have to talk about that now, there are more important things to deal with than your love life.' His tone was harsh, he was hurt, and worse than that, I was the one that hurt him.

'You need to change before you meet Kai, there are some clothes inside for you. Meet me out here when you're ready,' he quickly changed the subject, so I didn't have the opportunity to say another word to him about it. I just nodded in agreement and walked back toward the warehouse, following his instructions, not wanting to continue our conversation any more than he did.

We sat in silence for the entire journey to meet Kai, both of us were lost deep in our own thoughts. When we arrived, I found myself mesmerized by the size of the building, it was a *castle*. Not exactly the most subtle headquarters. It stood around 100 feet tall, with a breathtaking mountain landscape encasing it. To the right of the castle lay more forest that seemed to stretch for miles, it was truly stunning. Although it was hidden deep in the mountains, if anyone drove by they would surely see it.

'How has no one found this yet?' I asked in amazement.

'It's invisible to them, we can make certain things invisible to the human eye and the other races for protection,' Ezra answered me, still no expression showing on his face and his tone dry. His hands gripped the steering wheel tighter, so the whites of his knuckles were now showing, and he didn't take his eyes off the road once, seeming to answer only as a formality. I know very little about the abilities we have, we don't receive them until we reach our eighteenth birthday and since I was sent to Earth just before, I never got the chance to find out how they worked.

Ezra parked beside the castle and walked quickly around the jeep to open my door, I stepped out as he held his hand for me to take. It took me by surprise that he was choosing now to be affectionate when he had spent the entire journey being cold. I wrapped my fingers around his, not wanting to shrug off his gesture, I figured I'd already caused him enough hurt for one day. It was almost as if he was pushing away what I had told him at the warehouse. Like if he didn't talk about it with me, it wouldn't exist. Greyson wouldn't exist. When my hand united with his and I felt his warmth, it was noticeably different to how Greyson's hand felt in mine. It brought with it memories, of our past, a past I didn't have with Grey. I felt that rush of guilt again, though instead of dropping Ezra's hand I grasped him tighter. I know I should have refused his advance, but I couldn't, does that make me a bad person? I really don't know any more, I love them both, so I guess it does.

Ezra led me through the entrance of the castle, two wooden doors towered over us as we crossed the threshold, Ezra nodded to a man and a woman holding guns that smiled back in acknowledgement to him. It was hard not to feel overwhelmed at the sheer size of this place. We walked down six or seven concrete steps into a large gravel courtyard. Trees lined it in a perfect square with benches perched underneath each one. I looked up to the clear blue sky and then counted the floors, five. As we reached the far side of the courtyard, we were greeted by a grand stone staircase with a red runner darting along the centre. The walls were the same stone that encompassed the entire building. I sighed when I looked at how steep the steps were compared to the ones we had just walked down. The staircase twisted, breaking between floors and then continuing. Of course, we were headed for the fifth floor.

By the time we'd reached the top I was noticeably out of breath, my left hand feeling slightly sweaty in Ezra's. I looked at him, half expecting him to be as out of breath as me, but he didn't even look like his breathing had increased even slightly. We walked along the unusually wide hallway and stopped when we reached the last wooden door. It wasn't like the others that lined the hall, they were all placed adjacent to one another. This door faced out toward the entire hallway and had two, what I presumed to be, guards standing at either side.

The guard standing to the right of the door nodded to Ezra and moved to open the door. He walked in front of us and gestured for us to follow, he announced our presence to a tall figure standing beside a fireplace and left with a final thud as the door slammed closed behind him. I jumped a little at the sudden sound echoing off the stone walls.

'Welcome,' the extremely tall slender man exclaimed, walking toward us with open arms. When he finally reached us, I could see he was not much older than Ezra, his black hair was slicked back, and his dark golden eyes seemed to shimmer in the light of the room. His skin was extremely pale, like he hadn't seen sunlight in years. He wasn't a very attractive man compared to Ezra, but he had something about him that was very intriguing.

'It's so nice to finally meet you Rosie,' he smiled kindly at me. Ezra let go of my hand and walked closer to greet him with a handshake.

'Rosie, this is Kai,' Ezra explained.

'Thought so,' I muttered under my breath. Ezra seemed so at ease around him. Although I found him intriguing, there was also something intimidating about him, maybe how tall he was or maybe it was the odd smile that tugged at his lips like it was being controlled by an invisible piece of string.

'Ezra has told me so much about you over the past few months, I feel like I already know you. I have quite a lot to talk to you about, I'm sure you also have lots of questions that I would be most delighted to answer, once I fill you in?' I nodded and walked to stand beside Ezra.

'Please take a seat,' Kai gestured at two red suede chairs facing him. It was an odd room, covered with medieval style portraits and deer heads; it was like the castle hadn't been redecorated in centuries. The large open fire rested to the right of the room and four small windows lined the wall adjacent to the door. The chairs faced toward the windows and you would have assumed there should have been a desk in front of them, instead there was just an empty space where Kai stood over us. His height even more apparent now that we were sitting. There was no doubt he was in charge.

'Let's see where I should start,' he hummed to himself.

'How much do you know Rosie?' Kai's eyes met my gaze and I suddenly felt uncomfortable facing his stare.

'Not much really, I left Atheria before I knew what was really happening.' I felt shame admitting that I had been sheltered from the war, when Ezra and clearly many others from Atheria had gone through so much pain.

'Ok then, I guess I should start with a brief summary to get you up to speed.' Kai moved toward the windows and perched himself on the ledge, he glanced to Ezra and then back to me, where he kept his gaze as he began to tell me about the war.

'It all started about ten years ago when a council member by the name of Xavier decided to move from Atheria and explore the other two worlds, like many of us do. Only Xavier took a small army with him and had other plans. He wants to build a better, stronger and more intelligent world. A superior race. He first took rule over Indira. From what we gather his motive is to learn each of the world's strengths and weaknesses so he can take the resources he needs and destroy anything that is useless to him. When he and his army invaded Indira they eliminated any of their leadership that refused to join him. Killing their entire lineage, men, women, and children were slaughtered at his hands. Their people were forced to join, or have their families tortured to death while they watched.' Kai stopped and looked at me before continuing. I felt my heartbeat pounding against my chest, Xavier had killed innocent people, children. I shuddered at the thought.

'I know it's a lot to take in Rosie, it's important that you know the history. Why your parents fought against Xavier's rebellion, and the value that holds,' he smiled softly, it seemed almost unnatural for him to convey such an emotion. He cleared his throat and continued.

'Next is Xavier's home, Atheria. When your parents and other council members heard what had happened on Indira, they started to form an alliance against him. Xavier returned to Atheria, with his now even larger army, and when some council members saw this, they deserted your parents and the rest of the council and joined Xavier.' Kai raised his eyebrow at the last sentence like he was judging them for fleeing their country. They had abandoned their people at the moment they needed them the most. The perfect definition of a traitor. I felt anger rise within me, if these people had stayed and fought for Atheria my parents and Ezra's parents might still be alive. But instead they chose a ruthless leader to follow for the sake of status and power.

'A lot of people were against joining a dictatorship with Xavier at the helm. Which divided Atheria, your parents had their loyal supporters, as did the other council members, but Xavier had the numbers. War was on the verge of breaking out when your parents sent you to Earth to protect you, knowing their uprising against Xavier had not grown as large as they had hoped and fearing the worst. They were right. The next three years were filled with pain and suffering, all at Xavier's hands. Your parents unfortunately lost their lives for this cause and that is why it is so important for us to continue their legacy and take Xavier down once and for all.' He breathed a sigh of relief, probably because he had finished his 'brief' summary of the war. I made a mental note to never ask Kai for a brief explanation ever again.

Kai's eyes locked on me, he looked as if he were studying my face to see how I had reacted to the revelation of the war I now found myself in the centre of. If only he could tell me how I was supposed to feel. The room felt tense after such a deep conversation, it was hard not to. My mind drifted back to everything Kai had just said. My parents had protected me from all of this, yet if they couldn't save themselves what chance did we really have?

Kai took a deep audible breath and broke the silence.

'So, I know that's a lot to take in, but time isn't something we have right now as I'm sure you'll understand. We need to know if you're on our side, more importantly, if you will join us and help to finish what your parents couldn't?'

Those last words stung, what my parents couldn't. I know he didn't mean it to, but it sounded like an insult that my parents were too weak for the fight. It almost insulted me that Kai had even asked me that question to begin with. Of course, I wanted to take Xavier down; he killed my parents, he killed Ezra's parents and countless other innocent people, I wanted to join the fight.

'Yes.' I spoke quietly yet firmly.

I felt a reassuring hand squeeze my arm. Ezra must have been able to tell by my reaction that I was having a hard time processing the knowledge Kai had just provided me with. I came in with so many questions I wanted answered, and now I had a million more, but for some reason I felt unable to create a simple sentence.

'I think that's enough for one day, I need to get Rosie

back to her human family,' Ezra intercepted Kai before he could respond to me.

'Yes, that's probably for the best, but bring her back as soon as possible; we need to start her training,' Kai replied rather sternly to Ezra, making his authority known. He seemed almost annoyed that Ezra had interrupted and called an end to his meeting.

We walked in silence to the car. I was still processing everything Kai had just told me. It doesn't bear thinking about if we lose this war. Kai's words lingered in the back of my mind, 'The next three years were filled with pain and suffering.' I couldn't help but think about Ezra, the scars on his face and arms, what he must of went through during those years.

We drove for hours before pulling into a small run-down hotel about three hours away from my human home. It was two in the morning and we both needed to rest. We approached the check in desk and the lady sitting perched behind it looked like someone from a film, and not in a good way. Her red lipstick was stained on her teeth, her dyed red hair was tied in a tight bow on top of her head and her long fingernails were painted in bubblegum pink. The smell of cigarette smoke lingered in the air. She looked down her nose through her glasses, staring at us one at a time before giving us a suggestive look with a raised eyebrow. Her assumptions couldn't be further from the truth. Ezra seemed oblivious to the woman's stares, either that or he was ignoring her. He paid in cash and the lady whose nametag read 'Dawn' pointed to our room before kindly asking we keep the noise down. Nice. Thanks Dawn. I looked at Ezra as he held open the door for me and his usual cool exterior had been replaced with slightly flushed cheeks. We reached our door, it was green I think, I could be wrong though it was covered top to bottom in grime. I flicked on the lights to see one large double bed in red. Yep, red. Just red. Literally red everything. The carpet, the headboard, the sheets, curtains, chair, walls, it was like someone had just come in and thrown red paint everywhere. Let's not even talk about the smell. Gosh, what kind of girl did she take me for? I laughed a little at that, and Ezra looked at me confused.

'Lovely, isn't it?' I mused.

He started to laugh, and not just a light chuckle, a full heavy laugh and I did too. Who would have thought Dawn's sleazy hotel would lighten the tension between us. We still hadn't spoken since the castle and I couldn't find the right words to say, but it turned out we didn't need words because laughter was enough to set things right.

Our laughter died down as we both lay on the bed, I looked up to see mirrors lining the ceiling, and there I was thinking it couldn't possibly get any tackier. When Ezra didn't speak, I decided to turn over and get some rest. I knew he was still upset about Greyson and we were merely hours away from seeing him. I closed my eyes when I felt Ezra's arms wrap around my waist, pulling me close to him. Without saying a word, we fell into a deep sleep.

I dreamt of us that night, of our childhood together, silly memories swayed around my unconscious mind reminding me how much in love with him I was and how much I still am. It was always him, no other boy had ever come close to how much I loved and cared for him. Even before I was old enough to understand what those feelings really meant. I was about to turn eighteen when my parents sent me to Earth and forged my new life, I knew then I only ever wanted to be with him for the rest of my life. Why did everything have to be so complicated now? Why did I fall in love with another man? I couldn't help feeling like I had betrayed them both. I always felt like something was missing from my life and Greyson filled that gap, but maybe he never did, maybe that gap was left because of Ezra, because on some level even with my memories erased, I still knew I would only ever belong to him.

Chapter 7

I opened my eyes startled awake by the loud banging coming from the door, nudging Ezra awake.

'Check out was at nine, you need to leave now!' A loud, very angry voice yelled into our room, Dawn.

Ezra jumped out of bed pulling the door open to face a very cross looking Dawn, now wearing a red floral dress. She was clearly the woman behind the decoration.

'We're leaving now,' Ezra replied coldly to her, turning to me and signalling for me to gather myself.

Dawn looked at Ezra, then to me, then back to him again, with a sinister smile making its way to her lips. The anger seemed to have gone instead she looked like she was judging us again, just like last night. I was pulling the jumper Ezra gave me over my head and then I heard her say, 'I'm sure you two had fun last night.' There she goes again with the accusations.

'Mind your own business,' Ezra said dryly, clearly having had enough of her.

'You're the one who brought a poor girl here at two in the morning boy,' she scoffed as she walked away. Ezra parted his mouth about to say something else when I grabbed his arm and pulled him out of the room past Dawn, down the hall, and out to his jeep.

We talked a little on the drive there and I even convinced him to stop for coffee. He didn't like the taste at all, I guess I had grown accustomed to it. Stanley, my human dad, always had a cup every morning and evening when he returned from work and it was something I'd joined in on. The closer we got though, the more the conversation between us started to fade. I knew the closer we got to home the closer we got to Greyson, and I felt a twist in my stomach.

We pulled into my driveway and a police car was parked on the footpath. I can only imagine what they've been going through, I felt so guilty. Ezra must have seen the look on my face because he grabbed onto my hand just before I opened the car door. He pulled me close to him and said, 'It's going to be ok, I'll explain everything to them.' He leant in and kissed me on my forehead, lingering a little longer than a friendly peck. We left the car as he walked with his arm around my waist. I knew I shouldn't let him. I knew it was wrong and had he been any other man I would have pushed him away and slapped him. But it wasn't any other man, it was Ezra.

'After you,' he said, signalling for me to open the door.

Taking a deep breath, I pushed open the front door and instantly heard a buzz of people talking as I turned in the hallway, Caleb caught my eye from the living room.

'She's home,' he yelled and ran over, picking me up in his arms and squeezing me tightly. His green eyes gleamed with excitement at my return. It wasn't long before the rest of the family followed. Mum, Dad and Greyson. They all seemed so happy and relieved I was home, each one taking their turn to hug me.

Greyson was the last one to greet me, wrapping his arms around me and pulling me close, his eyes seemed red like he was upset. Of course he was upset, I had been gone for five days without so much as a phone call. He'd probably assumed the worst, they all probably had. He leant in as if to kiss me and then looked up, glancing at Ezra who stood behind me. He pulled away quickly and asked, 'Who's he?' nodding toward Ezra with a confused look on his face. I knew where his mind was leading him. I wanted to comfort him, to tell him everything. Then, I looked around the room and everyone appeared serious, like they had gotten past the shock of my return and now they wanted answers.

How do I tell Greyson about Ezra? How are we going to explain this to them? The police officer waited patiently in the doorway, crossing his arms and frowning, waiting in anticipation for my explanation along with everyone else.

Ezra rushed to my side, wrapping his arm around my waist again and pulling me in closer against his body. 'I'm an old friend of Rosie's.' He smiled and looked only at Greyson. I think he was doing this on purpose, after Greyson's response to his presence.

Greyson glared at him. His eyes focused on Ezra's hand that was still placed on my waist and tensed his eyebrows in anger.

'Funny, I don't remember Rosie ever mentioning

you, do you know who he is?' he asked with his arms open, looking to the rest of my family.

This was Ezra's great plan? 'I'll explain everything,' he had told me. I guess he's worse at this than I expected. I was about to speak when a firm 'Yes,' echoed from my right. I turned and to my surprise it was Caleb. Why was he lying for Ezra? Greyson's glare now moved to Caleb and he looked angry, really angry.

'Ezra was Rosie's friend back in nursery, you remember, right Mum?' he looked at Mum and smiled.

'Oh … yes, I remember you now Ezra. You used to swap lunches with Rosie in nursery, how could I forget?' she smiled fondly at him.

How did she get that memory? I never once swapped lunches with anyone in nursery, actually I rarely went. We lived miles away from town so Mum only took me when she could afford petrol, and even that wasn't a real memory. I looked in front of me at Greyson, he seemed a little bit more relaxed now that my mum, Margaret, had suddenly remembered Ezra, though his eyes stayed fixated on Ezra's hand.

'Rosie, I need to ask you a few questions about the

past few days, and you too Ezra; the policeman interrupted Margaret's fond retelling of my nursery days. The one story had seemed to send her off on a tangent.

'I don't think that will be necessary sir,' Ezra stared at the officer.

'Ye … Yes … yo … you … are am right, I best get going now,' the officer replied stuttering and then hastily making his exit.

I looked around, waiting for someone to say something, but no one said anything. Everyone, including Greyson, seemed satisfied with the explanation that I had been staying with an old friend for the past few days and that they already knew about it. I guess Ezra could handle it after all.

I stood outside, looking up at the stars when I felt familiar hands wrap around me. 'I missed you,' Grey whispered gently. He spun me around to face him, taking my head between his hands. 'I missed doing this,' he pressed his lips against mine, working his way from my lips down to my neck and back to my lips. My hands held onto his neck as his moved down to my back holding me tightly against him. He pulled away from our embrace for a moment. 'Can I stay here tonight?' he asked, catching his breath.

It felt strange that my immediate response was not to say yes. I couldn't stop thinking about Ezra, we'd spent the past few nights curled up together sharing a bed. I suddenly felt awful. Greyson was my boyfriend and I had been sleeping next to another man, one I have very strong feelings for. Grey and I had been in a relationship for the past year, and before that we were close friends. I owed him to at least be honest, but how? What is safe for me to tell him? The truth is Greyson and I had never slept next to each other. I looked up and realised he was still waiting for a response while my thoughts had drifted.

'Yes,' I answered unsure, hoping he didn't hear the hesitation in my voice.

'I just don't want to say goodbye to you yet,' he whispered.

We spent the rest of the evening outside, curled up together on the deck chairs. I kept looking back over my shoulder to catch glimpses of Ezra. Greyson filled me in on all I had missed in the last few days, as I kissed him between silences, for a moment life felt normal again. It was nice to pretend everything was still as it had been just four days ago. Greyson didn't know about my parents and the grief I was dealing with; he didn't know I wasn't from Earth, and he didn't know about Ezra yet. That part filled me with the most guilt. It felt unfair that Greyson didn't know about Ezra's importance in my life. I made my way upstairs as Greyson and Ezra took off into the living room.

I tossed and turned for the remainder of the night. I couldn't stop this feeling in my stomach, it was almost like my feelings toward Grey were drifting away from me, just like my memories of my human life had. Did I love him? Yes, I did, of course I did, but was I in love with him? That was the problem.

I woke early the next morning and crept out of bed, walking slowly downstairs, careful not to wake anyone from their sleep. Ezra was already awake, the blankets he had used folded in a neat pile. He was now sitting on the deck chairs outside. I glanced down at Greyson who was fast asleep on the opposite sofa. I hesitated before I opened the patio door and stepped outside, tugging my light blue robe closed and keeping myself warm from the cool morning breeze. I sat down next to him without speaking.

'Lovely morning isn't it?' he said.

The weather, really? Is that what he wants to talk about? Why is he being so difficult? We have a million and one things to talk about and he chooses small talk.

'Yep, breathtaking,' I replied sarcastically.

'How'd you sleep?' he replied, obviously ignoring my previous sarcasm.

'Ok.' My tone was harsh, I was trying to figure out what he was getting at.

'Aren't you going to ask me how I slept?' he glared at me.

'Fine, Ezra how did you sleep?' I crossed my arms and waited for his response.

'Great, it was so considerate of you to invite *him* to stay.'

I tried not to smirk and failed.

'Glad you find this funny.' He averted my gaze.

'I didn't know it would be such an issue.' I chuckled.

'You love him, not me, there's no need to spare my feelings, but did you really need to invite him to stay.' My smile faltered as I took in the tone to his voice, he struggled with the words. As he looked right into my eyes, I could see the hurt in his piercing blue eyes. I hated what this was doing to him. I hated myself for doing this to him. How could I have been so stupid, of course that would have hurt him. I should have listened to my instincts and told Greyson to go home.

'That's not true.' The fact Ezra believed that I loved Greyson over him made me want to scream. Not at him, at myself. I was wedged between them both.

He shook his head in disbelief, 'There's no need to lie to me Rosie.'

'No, you don't get it, I—'

The patio door opened before he had a chance to respond to me, but he had a smug look on his face now. I can only imagine what reply he was conjuring up for later. Caleb slid the patio door closed behind him, being careful not to wake anyone else.

'That was a close one yesterday,' Caleb said, smiling at Ezra and taking the seat to his left.

'Wait, you know?' I asked Caleb, surprised.

'Of course I know. Wait, has Ezra not filled you in on everything yet?' he asked, giving Ezra a judgmental yet playful look. 'Hmm, I suppose he hasn't by the look on your face, what have you been doing for the past few days then Ezra? Let me guess, you're just so excited to have your Rosie back,' he chuckled to himself. 'Some things never change,' he laughed again rolling his eyes at Ezra.

'Does someone want to fill me in please?' I asked, glaring at both of them.

Ezra shook his head at Caleb and looked to me, 'Sorry Rosie, I should have told you before yesterday. Caleb is from Atheria too. He came here for protection just like you, only he also came to protect you. Caleb has been on Earth for just over two years now?' he looked to Caleb for reassurance, Caleb nodded in response and Ezra continued.

'He spent a year with me while we were, well you know, going through everything. He was a prisoner with me. When he was released, he went to Earth, looked for you and merged himself into your family, creating his own place in your memories as your older brother, to protect you, for me.'

'Oh, I see,' I said, shocked at his explanation, but it now made sense that those memories for the last two years with Caleb remained real in my mind.

Greyson pulled open the door yawning and walked over to sit beside me. Ezra gave him a look that in that moment

I was grateful looks could not actually kill someone. He didn't like Greyson and he wasn't shy about showing it.

'I need to get freshened up and then we can go see Libby, right Cal?' I gestured to Caleb, trying to distract from the tension that now shadowed us.

'Yeah sure, she's really missed you, we can bring Ezra along too. I'm sure he wants to see some more of your new life?' He smiled smugly, knowing exactly what he was doing.

It's strange that only four days ago Caleb was my older brother, debatable best friends with my boyfriend and dating my best friend. It had been simple. Well, maybe simple wasn't the right word but we were human then. Now he's my kind of ex-boyfriend's best friend, his relationship with Grey remains uncertain and whether or not he actually cares about Libby or me also remains unknown.

I stood in the shower for a lot longer than I needed to; feeling the heat of the water trickling down my skin was soothing to know that, although my life had just got a lot more complicated, some things were still the same. Today was my last day of being 'human', then Ezra was going to remove their memories of me and Caleb so we could meet with Kai and train for the impending battle. Today I was going to have to say goodbye to them, forever.

I threw on a mustard coloured dress with cap sleeves falling just below my knee. I wore my long curly hair down, not bothering to fix it. I took one last glance at myself in the mirror and sighed. Although everything in my life had changed, I still looked the same. I walked downstairs to all three men waiting patiently for me. Grey took my hand and walked me to Ezra's jeep.

We arrived at Libby's house and she was already half-way to the car when we pulled up, she must have been waiting for us. I jumped out of the car to greet her. She hugged me and spun in circles with excitement to see me.

'Come on in, you have to tell me all about your trip.'

She ran and greeted Caleb with a kiss before noticing Ezra.

'Who *is* this?' she asked raising her eyebrow at me.

'Ezra, he's an old friend Lib.'

She nodded knowingly and grinned.

'Friend … if that's your story,' she lowered her voice so

only I could hear, and I felt a blush appear on my cheeks. Libby was a live wire, there's no better way to describe her, she loves life and lets everyone know it. She has this amazing quality of lifting everyone's mood within a moment. She is an incredible person, even with our childhood memories taken away I have a feeling we would still be friends without all that. She is insanely beautiful too with long red hair, little freckles covering her nose and cheeks, her skin was like porcelain and her wide hazel eyes shone against it. If I told everything to Libby, she would be crazy enough to believe me without hesitation.

After a few hours of catching up, it was time to say goodbye and go back home. Greyson left to spend some time at his parents' house for the evening since he had pretty much been waiting at mine for me to return home the past few days. The car ride was silent back to our house. Ezra was tasked with helping my dad repair his car, after expressing his interest in cars earlier during the day, I did warn him. Caleb and I sat outside together, asking each other questions and basking in the sunlight. It's weird that I still feel like he's my big brother, even after learning everything. If anything, I feel closer to him now that we can be honest with each other.

'Can I ask you something Cal?' I sighed, knowing I wanted to ask the question yet also knowing I was not going to like the answer that accompanied it.

'Of course, isn't that what we've been doing?' He smiled and chuckled a little, encouraging me to continue.

'What happened on Atheria, to Ezra I mean, what happened to him?' I pushed the words out as quickly as possible before I lost the courage.

'You're not going to like this, are you sure you want to hear it?' he asked, questioning me with concern in his tone.

'Please I just ... I just need to know Caleb.' I stuttered a little, bracing myself for what I was about to learn.

'It wasn't a good place to be, that's why your parents got you out. Ezra's parents were too late and he insisted on staying with them anyway. You know him, always doing the right thing. I was with him for the first year and we became friends quickly, he's a hard guy not to like. But when they killed your parents and his, they made a spectacle of it. It was a lesson, if you rebel against Xavier this is what will happen. They tortured them for days and then they murdered them, making him and all who followed them watch, it was horrible. He got in a lot of trouble after that, I think you were the only thing that made him keep fighting. They tortured him and used him as another example. I'm truly surprised he managed to survive nearly three years of it, if it wasn't for Kai he wouldn't have escaped. When I got a way out, I promised him I'd find you, keep you safe until he could be with you again. I really didn't think he would ever get the chance after the last beating he took. It was bad, really bad. He kept a picture of you two in his pocket and I really believe you got him through it somehow.' He looked into my eyes and I couldn't hold back the tears any longer as I started to cry. Caleb jumped up from his chair and knelt on his knees, pulling my head to his chest and rubbing my back.

'I told you it wasn't good,' he sighed.

'I feel awful.' Tears kept trickling down my cheeks, I wasn't one to often cry easily but knowing what Ezra and Caleb both had had to go through broke my heart.

'All this time, he was going through all that and then when he gets here, he has to deal with all of this.' I raised my arms, gesturing. Caleb wiped away my tears with the sleeve of his jacket.

'You weren't to know. Your real memories were taken

from you. But you do need to make a decision, it's not fair on either of them. You know Grey and I are friends too. I do like him, but my loyalties lie with Ezra. I care about you too Rosie, I might not be your real brother, but I feel the need to protect you, like I would my own sister. I see the way you look at Ezra and I also see how you look at Grey. To me it would be an easy decision, but it's not mine to make. Only you know how you really feel.'

I nodded, acknowledging him. *How I feel*, the truth is I had no idea how I felt. The only thing I knew I did feel was a need to find Xavier and kill him for what he did to our parents and what he did to Ezra, Caleb and our people.

Ezra finished helping my dad repair the car and returned to join me and Caleb. Our parents left for the evening, so we had the house to ourselves to discuss erasing their memories of us. I know I was never supposed to be a part of their lives, but I like having them. I like having a family, a mum, dad, and a brother who love me. I miss my parents, my real parents and I just don't know if I'm ready to say goodbye to more people yet. Then there was another question on my mind. What about Greyson and Libby?

'Are we leaving for Kai first thing tomorrow morning?' Caleb spoke to Ezra.

'Yes, I think that's for the best. It still gives us tonight to get prepared and remove you both from their lives.'

I watched them converse with each other, still lost in my own thoughts. They hadn't mentioned Greyson or Libby yet. I couldn't help but wonder what Grey would think if I told him the truth. Would he still love me? I'm not the person he fell in love with anymore, my past, my likes, ambitions, they were all someone else's, not my own. Sadness drifted over me, what would my life be like without him? What if they do remove our memories, our real memories we shared together, and I become a stranger to him? I couldn't bear the thought any longer.

'What about Greyson and Libby?' I said, interrupting them and hoping for the answer I wanted so desperately to hear.

Ezra looked to me and studied my face as if he were reading my thoughts, 'I hadn't really thought about them.'

'I don't want to remove myself from Libby's life, if that's ok with you two. I do however want to keep her out of this as much as possible,' Caleb responded quickly, I could hear the desperation in his voice.

'That's ok with me, I don't want to remove myself from Grey's life either,' I kept my gaze on Ezra, who now looked worried.

'If neither of you want to remove their memories of you, you need to tell them the truth. We can take your parents' memories away and leave theirs. You will be putting them both in danger by telling them though, it's your choice.' Ezra replied coldly, turning his back on us and walking to the kitchen.

Caleb shook his head at Ezra's abruptness, 'Don't listen to him Rosie, he's just hurt that you still care about Grey. I'm going to tell Libby now. Do you want a lift to Grey's house?' Caleb brushed off Ezra's warning, smiling at me.

'Please,' I replied softy.

All I could think about for the entire car journey was how I was going to explain everything to Greyson without sounding crazy. Humans are the only race that are unaware of the other two worlds. Which also means they are the least likely to believe a twenty-one-year-old girl claiming she's from another planet. One thing was certain, this was not going to be easy. As we pulled into Greyson's driveway, I could see his family eating their usual Sunday dinner together, all five of them were nestled around the dark wood oval dining table. I took a deep breath and thanked Caleb for dropping me off, wished him good luck and stepped outside of the car.

chapter 8

I sat tensed on the edge of Greyson's bed, watching him pacing up and down the length of his bedroom, waiting patiently for his next question.

'And Ezra?'

'He's from Atheria,' I answered.

'Have you known him a while then?'

'Yes,' I replied, hoping if I kept my answer short, he would stop asking questions about Ezra, but I had a feeling he wasn't going to let me off so lightly.

'How well do you know him?' He had stopped pacing and stood adjacent to me, his eyes narrowing.

'We've been best friends since we were children.' I stopped mid-sentence, afraid to say anymore.

'Did you ... did you ever go out with him?' His voice now sounded hoarse, like he needed to clear his throat.

'Yes.'

'For how long?'

I knew exactly what he was doing and it amazed me that merely an hour ago I had walked into his house, disturbed his family's weekly dinner, took him to his room and told him everything I had learnt in the last few days, and the biggest question on his mind was if I still had feelings for Ezra. Maybe he was the crazy one.

'Two years. I was almost eighteen when my parents sent me to Earth, so we were together for just over two years until then,' I hoped if I gave him a slightly longer answer he would move on. His eyebrows tensed and he looked away as though deep in thought.

'So, you never broke up?' He sounded concerned.

'No.' This time I gave a one-word response, not because I didn't want to talk to Greyson about Ezra, but because it was the first time I realised that Ezra and I never broke up. We never ended it, and I doubt that if I had stayed on Atheria we would have ever ended our relationship. I suddenly felt overwhelmed and a knot twisted in my stomach.

'Do you still love him?' Greyson's voice abruptly intercepted my thoughts.

Do I still love him, how do I answer a question like that to my boyfriend? I came here to be honest with him because I didn't want to remove his memories of me, because they were real. I didn't want to lose him just like Caleb didn't want to lose Libby. The only way we can keep them in our lives is to be honest with them, but where do we draw the line? If I was going to be honest and tell Grey everything, I would tell him that I could never stop loving Ezra, that I just know I will love him for the rest of my life, that when I got my memories back, he was all I wanted, all I needed. How do I tell my boyfriend that not only do I still love him, but I am still in love with him? I love Grey too, and that's the problem. I know I can't have them both, but I need them both in my life. As horrible and selfish as that seems, I can't lose them, not when everything else is falling apart.

I took a deep breath and answered Greyson's question as honestly as I could, hoping I wouldn't hurt him with my words yet knowing it was inevitable.

'Yes, I do, but please Grey, I love you.'

'You love him?'

'Grey, please.'

'So, when you were in the warehouse just after you got your memories back, you knew you loved him?' he asked, his voice loud and angry.

'I ... y ... yes,' I stuttered.

'And when you stayed in the hotel with him, you knew you loved him?'

'Grey ... I ...'

'Where did you sleep Rosie?'

'What do you mean?'

'In the hotel, where did you sleep?'

My heart thudded against my chest as it picked up pace. I knew what he was getting at and now I felt angry. Angry at him for thinking I would just cheat on him and angry at myself for being so stupid and hurting him.

'In bed.'

'Where did *he* sleep?' he asked, a bitter tone to his voice.

I took a deep breath and exhaled, knowing how this was going to sound. If only Dawn could see me now.

'Beside me ... but it wasn't like that I promise.'

'Oh ... you *promise*!' He started to yell. I've never once seen him this angry, I mean he'd get annoyed if I took the last donut but that was a playful kind of angry, this certainly wasn't. He was full on out of his mind enraged and I couldn't say I blame him.

'I can't ... I can't believe you Rosie. I can't believe you would do this to me. You came here and told me a lot of things that any other person would have laughed in your face for and I believed you because, I would believe anything you tell me no matter how crazy it sounds. Then you tell me that you are still in love with him after spending days alone together, but I'm supposed to be ok with it because you love me too?'

'I'm sorry.' Those words didn't feel like enough. They didn't truly represent how I felt. By Grey's reaction they didn't seem to be of any comfort either.

'I need time. I need time to process this Rosie. You can't expect me to just accept all of this. You are a different person now. Please just go.'

'What?'

'Go!' A harsh tone echoed in his voice. He stormed over to his bedroom door and held it open.

I left his room as fast as I could, and he slammed the

door quickly behind me. I passed his mum and little sister on my way out. His mum gave me an apologetic glance, indicating she must have heard us argue. Clearly, she didn't hear our actual argument though or she'd be throwing her shoe at me. I ran quickly out the front door and I couldn't hold it in any longer, tears filled my eyes and trickled down my cheeks. I covered my mouth with my hand to stop anyone hearing me and then I felt warm arms stretch around my body and pull me in, Caleb. I rested my head against his chest, as I tried to control my breathing.

'What did he say?' Caleb asked as he held onto me tightly.

'He was upset. He told me to leave,' I buried my head deeper into Caleb.

Caleb pulled my chin up so that my eyes would meet his gaze, I could see the all too familiar flicker of anger in his eyes. I glanced away from him for a moment and that's when I noticed Libby standing slightly behind him with her eyebrows furrowed in concern.

'Stay with Libby,' he ordered.

'Just leave it Cal. It … It's ok,' I was trying to prevent

Caleb from making this whole mess worse.

He ignored me and strode off into Greyson's house without bothering to knock first.

Caleb returned after what felt like a lifetime, without saying a word to either of us he walked toward his car, gesturing for us to follow. He drove quickly home, opting to drop Libby off on the way. She had wanted to see me after finding everything out but after how Grey took the news, I wasn't in much of a mood to talk, so she kindly went back to her house instead of ours. There was only one thing left to do now. Say goodbye to my parents, remove their memories and move into the castle to begin training. That was the plan. I just didn't know how I was going to remove my human parents from my life. They wouldn't remember anything about me or Caleb. I tried to remind myself that this is how it was meant to be, they were never meant to have two children in their lives and things would go back to its normal order, as it was intended. But they are the closest thing I have to parents in any world, and I just don't think I am ready to say goodbye. I wish the choice was mine to make.

When we arrived at the house Caleb filled Ezra in on what had happened with Greyson and Libby. As Caleb told Ezra about Greyson, he looked at me and to my red blotchy eyes, giving me a soft comforting smile. He had seen me cry a lot in these past few days, I usually wasn't one to cry easily but I guess these were exceptional circumstances. We sat down on the sofa, sitting next to each other as Caleb put on a film. We just needed to wait until Stanley and Margaret were asleep; it was easier done while they slept. Caleb seemed engrossed in whatever action movie he had opted for, usually we tossed a coin to decide who picked the film, but I guess this wasn't one of our usual nights. Ezra seemed to be distracted like I was, though I doubted our thoughts were anything similar to one another's.

'Let's get this over with so we can leave.' Ezra edged off the sofa and stood. It was past midnight now so the probability that both Stanley and Margaret were asleep was high. I nodded in agreement leaving Caleb and Ezra to discuss the finer details and gathered a few pieces of clothing in a black duffle bag to take with me. I entered

Mum's bedroom, both her and my dad slept beside each other. Margaret and Stanley, I reminded myself. I sat gently on the edge of their bed and said something that I never got to say to my real parents, goodbye. It broke my heart to leave them, to allow Ezra to remove their memories of us but I had to do it. This wasn't about me anymore. Their safety was more important, I couldn't risk them losing their lives because of me. I walked past Ezra entering their bedroom, glancing back over my shoulder to watch him close the bedroom door. As I came down the stairs Caleb raised his hand and motioned over his shoulder toward the door.

'Let's get out of here.' The side of his mouth lifted in a slight smile. He might not be my real brother, still he was the closest thing to it.

Chapter 9

I t was dark as we pulled up to the castle, the moon served
as a perfect backdrop to the picturesque setting. Ezra
opened my door and took my hand, leading me toward the
entrance, as Caleb followed closely behind. As we entered,
we were greeted by a girl about my age, maybe a year or
two younger with a dark black pixie haircut and eyes as
dark as the night sky. She greeted us and introduced herself
as Alena.

‘Glad to see you back, and here I was thinking you were
slacking off in your duties,’ she said laughing. Ezra smiled
back at her as she gestured for us to follow.

‘Kai asked me to show you to your suite, since it's late

he thought it best to begin training in the morning. Ezra, can you show them around tomorrow?'

'Sounds good.'

She led us up to the fourth floor of the castle and down a dimly lit corridor. I was glad that we were only going to the fourth floor this time. Ezra walked closely beside me, still holding my hand. I liked that he hadn't let go of me yet, but I couldn't help but think how different this would have been had Greyson been here. I held out hope that he would come around and somehow find me, but as much as I hoped, I knew it was very unlikely. He knows how I feel about Ezra now, how will he ever move past that? I have to put my feelings for both of them aside and focus, I need to focus. I let go of his grasp, I guess it just felt so natural; half the time it didn't even seem like he realised he was doing it. He noticed when I dropped my hand from his and gave me a look, one that I can't describe as anything other than pain.

'This is your suite, Kai said you would all prefer to stay together?'

Alena interrupted my thoughts as I entered through the doorway. A small oak dining table lay to the right with four chairs surrounding it, with a large slightly worn brown leather sofa in the middle of the floor. A green Persian rug framed the coffee table in front of it, and a television sat directly across from the sofa, with a very well-loved green armchair to the side. The furniture looked odd in a room this size. The room was lit by the same dim lighting as the hallway and two small windows were framed by the same stone that consumed all four walls. An open fireplace sat opposite the sofa keeping the room warm. Three dark wooden doors slipped off the main living room, one bathroom, one bedroom with a king size bed and one bedroom with two double beds. Alena walked to the first bedroom and pushed the door open wide.

'This is Ezra and Rosie's room, Kai said you two would want to be together. Caleb, you can have this room,' she pointed toward the door on the far right.

'Breakfast is at six in the main hall and training starts at seven so don't be late,' she excused herself and left the suite, closing the door firmly behind her.

Ezra walked into the bedroom with the king size bed and placed my bag on top of it. I hadn't even noticed he had been carrying it until now.

'I'll sleep in the other room with Caleb,' he said, turning to leave.

'Wait.' I don't know why I said it, but I couldn't help myself.

He turned to face me, waiting to see what I was going to say next.

'Thanks.' That's the best I could come up with. I wanted to ask him to stay, to talk to him like we used to. When something big happened he was always the first person I'd go to, though I guess he wouldn't want to hear about this.

The next morning arrived all too quickly. I followed Ezra and Caleb into the breakfast hall, long wooden tables were spread across the hall, each with an array of food, everything you could imagine was lined along the centre of each table. From fruit, to breads, to cooked breakfast, everything. There was a refrigerated area at the far end of the room that seemed to have prepacked food and drinks. I sat down and filled my plate, starving, I guess with everything happening I had forgotten to eat. Caleb and Ezra watched in amazement while I tucked into my mountain of food as Caleb started to laugh.

'Slow down there, you might want to save some for the rest of us,' he said chuckling.

I rolled my eyes at him, gesturing to the amount of food on the table with my fork.

'I think there's enough,' I said sarcastically.

After we ate together, we made our way to the training room. To say it was massive would be a complete understatement. It panned halfway across the bottom floor of the castle with no windows; it was lit only with artificial light. Although the rest of the castle was obviously outdated, the training gym was filled with advanced technology which surprised me. It seemed to be divided into four sections: combat, strength, weaponry, and lastly, abilities. The last section interested me the most as it seemed to work with each individual's abilities, training them to be used in war. Seeing this room and seeing these people, the people I will be fighting beside in a matter of months, brought everything home, making me realise this is really happening, we are going to war, that much is inevitable. It will happen, the question is when.

'We will start you both off here, I need to see where you are both at.' Ezra stood beside two large punching bags and pointed for us to stand at each one.

As I started throwing punches against the bag, I realised I was terrible. Actually no, I was worse than terrible, I was a disaster. I had never punched anything, not once in my life and it was obvious. Physical fitness wasn't exactly on my agenda in university either. Ezra watched without saying a word as I moved onto each one of the sections, except abilities. He kept a close eye on me at all times. I kept waiting for him to say something, but he just watched. His face gave nothing away of what he might of been thinking. He seemed to hold a high authority amongst the others, they interrupted our training to ask him for advice on techniques from time to time. We didn't finish until past seven in the evening and by that time I needed to sleep. I walked slowly to our suite, my legs aching under me. The training didn't seem to faze Caleb at all. I suppose he had kept up to par whilst living with the humans.

'Don't you want anything to eat?' Ezra asked looking worried.

'No, sleep ... I just need sleep,' I yawned, walking to my room and closing the door tightly behind me. I collapsed headfirst onto the bed and for the first time fell asleep immediately.

Chapter 10

I opened my eyes taking in my surroundings and for a brief moment I was unsure of where I found myself. Then the events of the last week flooded back to me. I rolled over onto my right side, glancing at the small clock perched on the nightstand, it was nearly six in the morning. I forced my feet outside of the warm sheets and onto the icy concrete floor, wincing slightly at the sudden coldness against my bare skin. I rushed to get dressed as quickly as possible, knowing it was likely that Caleb and Ezra had been up for a while and would be waiting outside for me to join them for breakfast. I pulled my navy jacket on over my t-shirt and tied back my loose curls into a slightly messy ponytail, then headed for the door.

I was right. Caleb and Ezra were both already awake and sitting on the sofa deep in conversation. As I walked over to them, I felt a glimmer of hope for our future. That one day when this war was over things just might return to normal. I was a little terrified by the thought of the impending war. The training I was undertaking only intensified that fear. When I had looked around the training gym yesterday and had seen the many different faces from Atheria, I couldn't help but wonder which of us would make it, and the leader in me wanted to say all of us. Though I knew that was naïve. In war there are no true winners, everyone loses something. That's my biggest fear, losing more of the people I love.

'Rosie,' Ezra stood up, greeting me.

'Are you ready to start training?' Caleb jumped to his feet. A spring in his step already and it's not even six yet.

'Yep, but first breakfast,' I mumbled, still half asleep.

Caleb lifted a plate off the coffee table with a bagel on it and passed it to me.

'You can eat this on the way, I want to get a head start on training before it gets overcrowded.'

So much for the big breakfast I had been dreaming of, I lifted the now cold bagel and sighed.

Alena greeted us in the hallway, her eyes glanced over Caleb and me before settling on Ezra and she looked relieved.

'Kai needs to speak with you,' she said with her gaze on Ezra.

Ezra turned to say something to Caleb that I couldn't hear, and Caleb gestured for us to keep walking. I watched as Ezra and Alena drifted out of sight and then continued walking down the long staircase to the training gym with Caleb.

'So, Ezra wants me to train you,' Caleb said, standing beside the punching bags. His lips were turned upwards in a slight smirk.

'What are we doing first then?' I asked, afraid to some extent by his expression.

'Well let's see what you've got against a real person,' Caleb nodded toward a large padded mat where two men were fighting, with their fists. Great.

After many, many attempts to fend off Caleb's attack I hit the padded floor again. It was just as well it was padded, otherwise I probably wouldn't be in good shape right now. I felt like a complete failure; everyone I had watched yesterday had fought equally, sure there were times when their opponent got the upper hand but for the most part it was a fair fight. There was no denying I was terrible. Even Caleb's usually cool exterior looked concerned. I guess everyone had been training for the last few years and physical fitness was something they exceeded in, I was letting everyone down.

'That's enough hand to hand combat for today, let's see how strong you are.' Caleb walked over toward the strength section of the training gym. It mostly consisted of weightlifting, pull up bars, leg and arm machines and weight racks. There were a few other pieces of equipment I didn't recognize. The only reason I knew what some were called was because I had been to the gym once, when Greyson invited me. I opted out of any future visits after that.

Surprisingly I didn't embarrass myself too much with the weights, maybe that one time with Greyson did come in useful after all. I had a feeling though that Caleb was going easy on me after how awful combat training had gone. We left the weights and moved onto shooting practice, my aim was off, way off. I'm pretty sure I hit the wall more times than the actual target.

'Ok, I think we will call it a day.' Caleb sounded even more exhausted than me.

He stayed in the training gym after I left for our room, he must have wanted to get some training in himself. I wasn't a very good training partner, that much was apparent. How was I ever going to survive this war? I was looking forward to learning about the abilities when Caleb called it a day. I wondered why he hadn't tried it when he had tried everything else with me. I stopped by the main hall and grabbed a tray of prepacked food to take back to my room. I hadn't planned on sticking around, but then a boy approached me. He was around my height and age with grey eyes and light brown curly hair, a friendly smile tugged at his lips.

'Hey, you're new here right?' he asked, curious.

'Yeah, I'm here with Ezra and Caleb.'

'Ezra, we all know him. He's the best soldier we have. What table are you sitting at?'

'I was actually planning on taking this back to my room to get an early night,' I added truthfully.

'You can eat with us if you'd like?' He gestured to a table with two girls and another boy.

Of course he knew Ezra, who didn't around here, it was like he was the golden boy of the castle. I really hoped they hadn't seen how my training was going. I nodded accepting his offer and followed him to the table.

'I'm Liam by the way,' he smiled.

'Rosie,' I smiled back, maybe making some friends would be good for me.

'Hey guys, this is Rosie. She's new,' Liam said as he sat down, immediately reaching for food to fill his plate.

'Hi Rosie, I'm Annora, you can call me Nora,' a girl with a dark complexion and long wavy dark brown hair smiled.

'That's Heather and Knox,' Liam said, gesturing to the two other people sitting in front of me. Heathers short blonde hair was styled with a fringe, little freckles dotted around her face, clustered together. Knox's hair was shaved to his scalp, showcasing a tattoo, his eyes fixated on me, 'I watched you train today,' He said with a slight laugh.

'Leave her alone Knox, it was her first day,' Liam paused for a moment, looked at me and then said slightly nervously, 'Right?'

I could feel my cheeks redden; they had seen the embarrassment that was today.

'Yes' I replied sheepishly.

'See, I told you,' Liam confirmed.

Knox rolled his eyes, 'It was still the worst I have ever seen from someone in here.'

'Stop being a jerk Knox,' Nora chimed in and gave me an apologetic smile.

'What, I'm just saying what everyone's thinking,' he said defensively.

'You can't say that to her Knox,' Heather's voice sounded shocked as she glared at him, giving him a look of warning. This just keeps getting more and more embarrassing. To say I'm regretting sitting down would be an understatement.

'Why not?' he looked at Heather dead in the eye, confused.

'Her name is *Rosie*,' she exaggerated my name and gestured her head, nodding it toward me. It's as if I didn't exist, the way they were talking. This was getting more than a little uncomfortable.

'Yes *Heather*, I gathered her name is *Rosie,* and that's important why?' He moved his hands, encouraging her to continue.

'She's a founding family member you idiot,' Heather finally gave up and rolled her eyes.

Oh, *that's* how they know me. I guess spending all

this time away from home had made me forget just how important my family were there. Things are so different on Earth, yet similar in ways. She was right though, Atheria's government consisted of five council members lead by two representatives from the two founding families, mine and Ezra's. It's similar to some of Earth's government systems, only with two families at the top instead of just one. This was to try and keep opinions as democratic as possible. And with the three other council members, it meant everyone's opinions and concerns were always heard. It kept our world peaceful, or so we thought.

'Oh,' Knox's cheeks turned a bright shade of red.

'I'm sorry, I didn't mean to. I mean, I'm sure you'll improve?' he choked on his words.

Laughter took over me, 'You weren't wrong. I *was* terrible.'

Knox started laughing with me and then Liam and the girls joined in. Once our laughter had settled down the mood lightened and the rest of the dinner went well, we chatted back and forth, and I started to feel a sense of normality again. It reminded me of university with Libby, if only she were here. I learned that Nora and Knox were a couple and Heather had an on-off romance with a guy called Wyatt, who she was now completely over, or so she assured Nora and me many times. They started to ask about Ezra, and that's when I decided to leave.

The next two weeks went by quickly and I was happy with the progress I had made during training. I was now at least blocking some of Caleb's punches and managed to control a few with some of the techniques he had shown me. I was lifting heavier weights and I could feel that my body had strengthened when I used the other equipment. My aim was getting better too. I was hitting the target, which was a rather significant improvement from the time I almost shot Caleb. He had stopped our training early that day.

He still hadn't taken me to the ability section yet and I was starting to grow impatient. No one had explained our abilities to me and aside from what my parents had told me when I was younger, I really had no idea how it worked. Ezra had been like a passing ship the last two weeks. I would walk past him sometimes as he headed to training and I left with Caleb. I ate dinner with Liam and the rest of his friends each evening, Caleb had even joined us a few times until Heather started making advances. He either joins Ezra or sits with a few of the other groups now. Libby calls almost every day and spends hours on the phone with him. Caleb sometimes allows me twenty minutes with her before he grows impatient. He really does love her, and it's obvious how much he misses her.

I was starting to spar with Caleb when Ezra entered. I didn't even have to turn around to feel his presence in the room. He walked straight up to us, brushing off anyone trying to ask him questions.

'I want to see how much you've improved,' he said, as our eyes held each other's.

I kept taking hit after hit. I got a few punches in, which I thought Ezra would be pleased about, given how much I had improved in just a couple of weeks. I took another hit, this time knocking me down onto the padded mat.

'Stop.' Ezra's tone was serious.

'She's improved loads,' Caleb said, holding out his hand to help me up. I could tell he felt guilty about the punches, but it was the only way we would learn.

'If that's what you call improvement, then we have no chance,' Ezra voiced his concerns, his arms crossed tight against his chest, staring at Caleb.

'Look man, I'm telling you, another six to eight months and she will be good,' Caleb said, hopeful.

'We might not have six to eight months.' Ezra sounded tense.

'Well, what do you want me to do then?' Caleb said, sounding exhausted of all options.

'I'll train her,' Ezra looked at me, his eyes focused on were Caleb's fist had connected with my cheek. I could feel the burn and was certain it would bruise eventually.

'Meet me here tonight around eight?' It sounded more like an order than a question.

'Ok,' was all I could say. I didn't want to train with Ezra, from the glimpses and things I had heard from the dinner table Ezra was a skilled fighter, and I knew I couldn't match that. He was like a gladiator, and they practically worshipped him here, I was the laughingstock of the castle. Not exactly a good match. I enjoyed training with Caleb, because although he pushed me, he wasn't too hard on me, he gave me time and held back a lot, which I was thankful for.

I ate dinner with Caleb, I didn't want another lecture from Nora and Heather about who's available to date, and how good looking they thought Ezra was either. I still hadn't told them what had happened with us, I didn't want to deal with the questions. I still felt awkward when they talked about him like that, I felt defensive, which I know I had no right to be. He was no longer my boyfriend.

'Are you looking forward to training tonight?' Caleb quizzed.

I rolled my eyes. Of course I wasn't looking forward to it. Ezra and I had barely exchanged three words in the last two weeks, and most of that was today. He rarely even looked at me and seemed to avoid me at all costs. I couldn't really understand why he even wanted to train me, unless Kai had put him up to it, not liking that there was a weak one amongst us. Kai usually comes and goes from the training gym and I've caught him watching me and Caleb a few times. I wouldn't be surprised if he had told Ezra to try to help me improve. Kai hasn't spoken with me since the first time I met him, he's usually either in his office working on our defense strategies, in the training gym or sometimes he seems to leave the castle for a few hours. I have no idea what he does when he leaves but I guess Ezra probably knows. I could always ask him.

'No, can't say I am,' I answered truthfully.

'Come on, you and Ezra will work this out,' Caleb sounded hopeful.

'I wouldn't be so sure of that Cal,' I nudged some food around my plate.

'You know just as well as I do how much he cares for you, you need to get out of your head and stop overthinking,' he tried to reassure me.

'It's not just me overthinking, he's been dodging me since we arrived.'

'You hurt him,' Caleb looked up, catching my gaze.

'I didn't mean to,' I looked away from him and back down to my food, moving the same piece of lettuce back and forth again.

'Of course you didn't mean to, that's not what I'm saying. But you did nonetheless, if you had of listened to me about Greyson then this would all be fine,' he said in his 'I told you so' tone.

'Don't lecture me Cal. How was I to know your warnings and snide remarks about Grey were really because

I was from a different world and in love with another man,' I glared at him.

'Didn't I make it clear enough?' he said smirking.

'No Cal, you didn't. Stop trying to turn this into a joke. I've hurt them both and now I don't know what to do.' I shook my head letting out a groan and placed it in my hands. 'Well, what am I meant to do tonight? Should I try to talk to him?' It felt so strange to ask someone else for advice on me and Ezra. We always talked about everything together, this was the longest we had ever gone without speaking, I missed him and how things used to be.

'Definitely don't try talking to him about Greyson, you know as well as I do he'll come around in his own time. There's nothing changed between you and Grey, is there?' he asked, curious.

'No. Well, I don't know, I don't exactly have any way of contacting him.' My phone still wasn't working.

'Then just go train and leave. Don't give him false hope where there isn't any. If you're still with Grey and "love" him then just look at it like one of our training sessions, ok?'

I decided to ignore the way he had said love, 'Thanks Cal, you always talk sense into me.' I glanced at the large clock centered above the door to the dining hall, 'I've got to go, I'm already late.' I took one last bite and bolted for the door.

'Good luck,' he yelled after me.

I walked across the gravelled courtyard, passing a few people that were seated on the benches and made my way through the corridor, down the steps and into the training room. I wondered why Ezra had wanted to wait until everyone had left to train me; it seemed odd. Maybe he just didn't want me to embarrass myself any more than I already had. He stood in the middle of the room preparing equipment, presumably for us to use.

'You're late,' he said without even looking up.

'Sorry.'

'Let's get started,' he gestured toward the mat.

I let out a small moan and took my stance. He walked around me, examining my form, having him looking at me so intensely caused my heart to pick up pace.

'Too tense.'

'What?'

'You're too tense. You need to loosen up.' He walked behind me, lowering my arms. His touch sent a shiver through my body, he let his hand linger for a moment before he turned to face me. He was close, really close.

'Good, now hit me.'

'No thanks.' I shook my head.

'Rosie, we are here to train, now hit me,' he repeated.

'No, you're not even defending yourself,' I motioned to his casual stance.

'You need to hit me with all your strength. Channel that into your punch,' he advised.

I looked at him apprehensively, it felt unnatural. My body didn't want me to hurt him.

'I'll be ok, just hit me. I can't know where you need to improve, if I don't know how hard you can throw a punch.'

I sucked in a deep breath. He was right. We were here to train. I never felt this sick feeling in my stomach when I trained with Caleb though. If I wanted to learn, I had to do as he said. I hesitated and then threw a punch toward him, feeling my fist connect to his jaw. It felt awful and pain seared through my hand immediately after. Ezra didn't even move, not one inch from where I'd hit him. The only thing that gave away what I had just done was a slight red mark already appearing on his right cheek.

'I can work with that,' he said smiling. Why was he smiling when I had just punched him? I shook my head at him in disbelief.

The next few hours went by so fast I didn't even notice time passing. We sparred some more, then moved onto the weights and shooting practice. I was already making progress in these few hours, it felt as though I had come so much further than I had in the two weeks with Caleb. I wouldn't tell Cal that though. Maybe the empty room helped me concentrate or maybe Ezra just knew me better to know what would work with me. It was nice talking and working with him, it felt like we were home again.

He walked over to the ability section and took a seat. As I followed his lead, sitting down next to him.

'Finally! Are we going to work on ability training now?'

'Yes,' he smiled. It wasn't his usual smile, he seemed nervous.

'I need to explain a bit more about the abilities we have before we get to your specific gift. Our parents were both the founding families of Atheria, so they were gifted with certain abilities that the rest of our people don't have. Our abilities are the main difference between us and humans. Naturally we are stronger and faster. We can remove their memories and create new ones easily. That's how Caleb was able to join your family, and also you. We can also hide things from them, like this castle for instance. Lastly, we can manipulate their emotions, Xavier must have used this one a lot to get to where he is, most of us don't unless it's absolutely necessary. That brings me to us, and probably the reason Caleb has avoided this section.'

'You see, we seem to have even more of those capabilities, gifts, that only founding families possess. Usually it's one gift Rosie, with us it's more than that. Obviously, we don't know what yours are yet, I have the ability to heal other people, and also ...' he paused, studying my face, almost to see if he should finish what he was about to say, then he moved on.

'It's why Kai brought me here with him, when he helped me escape the prison, he knew me being here would help bring more of our people out. Some were hiding out of fear but once people heard that a founding family member was behind it, they came and joined the fight. Now we just need to figure out your ability.' He looked at me and reached his hand out for mine before suddenly retracting it.

I'm not sure I know what to say. I was curious as to

why Ezra and I were different. I wondered what my gifts might be and by the sounds it, Ezra had at least one more he didn't want to tell me about. Under usual circumstances I would have asked him, but our relationship just didn't seem there yet.

'Ok. So, what do I need to do?'

'We can start with the basic tests to see where there is any sign of an ability. So additional strength is already ruled out, based on your weight limit. The next is healing.'

'So you think my ability might be the same as yours?'

'There's some evidence that it might be, we seem to be able to—' he stopped abruptly again, catching himself before he said any more. What is it he's not telling me?

'What are we able to do?' I couldn't bite my tongue any longer.

'We will pick up here tomorrow, same time?' he was dodging me.

'Fine, but tomorrow you answer my question Ezra,' I said, serious.

Chapter 11

Another few weeks passed and Ezra still hadn't answered my question. We trained every evening for hours, my body had started to change, becoming more defined and stronger. It was nice to train alone with Ezra, not having people judge me for not being up to par quite yet. Though I was learning quickly, and I could tell he was impressed.

'Good,' Ezra exclaimed.

'That wasn't just good, that was amazing,' I smiled and held out my hand to help him up. I'd managed to knock Ezra down for the first time and I was feeling smug about it.

'Ok, it was *really* good,' he laughed shaking his head,

knowing I was going to gloat about it a little longer.

We had worked around all the sections in the gym, and I was now never missing when it came to shooting practice, hitting the centre of the target every time. I was increasing my weight limits each day and was able to block and control punches from Ezra, even managing to deliver a few punches myself. Ability training was more difficult, I was mastering my skills in the usual abilities, though so far nothing had shown up for any beyond that. I was disappointed and he knew.

'I'm going to take a shower, that's us for tonight.' Ezra broke my train of thought.

'I think I'm going to stay here a little longer.' I started walking back toward the punching bag.

'You sure? You've worked really hard tonight. You need to rest too,' he said, his eyebrows furrowed into a frown.

'Yeah, I just need to get some more practice in on my own,' I shrugged.

'See you later then,' he swung his training bag over his shoulder and headed for the staircase. Once he was out of sight, I let out a breath I hadn't even realised I was holding in.

I was throwing punches against the bag when my thoughts started drifting to Greyson. I thought about him more as each day passed, it had been five weeks now. The longest we've ever gone without talking. I wished he could be here too although, I knew how foolish that was. Even if he could, he was human, and we weren't, he couldn't exactly keep up with us even if he turned out to be exceptional for a human. I wondered if we would ever speak again and I shrugged that thought quickly out of my head, we have to speak again. We love each other and love isn't just something you can turn on and off. *Ezra*. His name entered my mind and I shook my head. No. I can't think about him, I have to think about Greyson. But why did it all of a sudden feel like I was forcing myself and Greyson together, it was like every last fibre of my body screamed at me for Ezra, though I couldn't rid myself of the guilt that surrounded Greyson. I had done what he asked, I'd left his house to give him the space he needed. Maybe I should have stayed. I should have hugged him, kissed him, reassured him that I loved him. But I couldn't, because that felt like a lie. Was it? Did I love Greyson? Or did I just love the idea of being human and living a simple mundane life. If I had never come to Earth, if this war didn't exist, who would I be with? A memory flashed in my mind of me and Ezra, before everything happened. How carefree we were. How in love we were. Stop. I want my mind to stop trudging up these moments that were now gone. It hurt more than any physical pain, it hurt right down to my core. I knew what I was going to have to do and I didn't want to.

The next evening, I went to the training gym with Caleb. I wanted to practise my new skills with a different partner, so I didn't get comfortable with Ezra's movements. Ezra thought it was a good idea and came down to watch. I was about to step onto the mat when I heard a familiar voice.

'Rosie.'

I stopped dead in my tracks, was I hearing things? Dreaming? I turned around on my heels.

'Greyson.'

He walked swiftly toward me and embraced me, pulling me close to his chest and wrapping his arms around my back. It felt different than any other hug we had shared before, almost desperate. I paused for a moment before returning the gesture. Why didn't this feel the same?

'I've missed you,' he whispered gently into my ear.

'I've missed you too,' I whispered back, holding him tighter. I felt a pull in my stomach like I was uneasy and broke apart from him. Why did I do that?

'I knew you'd come around,' Caleb said, walking up to Grey and swinging an arm over his shoulder. He started to show Greyson around, when Grey turned to me and said, 'We need to talk.' He didn't say it the way I thought he would, instead he sounded hopeful, and I felt that twisted knot in my stomach again. I suddenly became aware of Ezra's presence, and looked around only to see him making his way out of the gym and up the staircase. I ran after him, wanting to make sure he was ok.

'Ezra,' I puffed, out of breath, this castle really was going to be the death of me between the training and the stairs. He kept taking larger strides, but I pushed through, catching up with him and almost pushing him over in the process.

I ended up pushing him into a wall with my hand resting on his chest, 'Are you ok?' I asked him, he looked into my eyes as he brought his hand up to cover mine.

'Who do you think brought him here?' he said.

He had brought Greyson here for me because he knew how I felt, but how did he know I missed him?

'Why?'

'You need him.'

'I … I don't know what to say.'

'You don't have to say anything,' he gently lifted a loose curl and placed it behind my ear, letting his hand linger there for a moment.

We stood there for a little longer than we should have in that position. This hurt him. I wanted to say more, I wanted to say thank you for understanding, for putting me first like he always does. I was glad Greyson was with us now, but I was scared of what feelings I had for him and how he had now become part of a war that didn't concern him. Ezra was the one who finally broke away, leaving me to watch as he disappeared out of sight. My heart ached a little more as his footsteps moved further and further away from me.

When I re-entered the training gym my eyes locked with Greyson's. He was talking to Caleb and Liam, I assumed they were bringing him up to speed and showing him the equipment. I'm sure all of this was overwhelming for him, it was overwhelming for me and I'm not even human. As I approached, their conversation came to an end and Liam smiled, leaving me to Greyson and Caleb.

'You hungry?' I looked at Grey, knowing it was dinner time and how far he had travelled to be here.

'Always,' his mood was lighter than the last time I had seen him. He seemed to be at more ease with everything and I hoped our talk wouldn't change anything.

I introduced Greyson to the rest of the group and we ate together, mostly in silence. Greyson had his arm placed around my waist, which gained a raised eyebrow from Heather, clearly wondering what our deal was. After dinner it was time for training with Ezra. I filled Greyson in on our usual routine and he wanted to come with me to watch. I wasn't so sure how I felt about that, so I asked Caleb to come and mediate, just in case.

I arrived on time and half expected Ezra to have bailed, knowing Greyson was here, but he was waiting for me as usual. He glanced between Greyson and me, noticing our hands clasped together.

'Let's get started.'

We started with some hand to hand combat training,

then weights, weaponry, and lastly abilities. This was our usual sequence, but tonight Ezra was trying something different when it came to abilities. We didn't have much time left, that we knew of. Resolving the issue of my additional capability was obviously high on his list of priorities. Ezra led us to a small side room with a hospital style bed in the centre. Making his way to what looked like a medicine cabinet, he opened it, lifting out a small object before returning to my side. He gestured for me to sit on the bed and I followed his instruction. Greyson gave me a look, making sure I was ok, and I nodded. Even Caleb looked a bit concerned. Ezra was holding a syringe. It looked similar to the one he used to return my memories to me, only this time the serum was gold with red shimmering specks throughout it.

'This is going to test for some more powerful capabilities, are you ok for me to use this Rosie?'

'Go for it,' I was willing to try anything to find out if I had any other abilities.

He moved closer to me, removing the small cap at the tip of the needle and I braced myself for the sharp sting. As it pierced my skin I looked down, noticing Ezra was now holding my hand, rubbing the top of it gently with his thumb, before my eyes closed.

When my eyes opened, I was home. And not home as in 54 Lotland Drive. Home as in Atheria. Ezra was still holding my hand, though this time instead of a hospital bed, it was a double bed covered in white and blue bedding. My old room. Ezra looked away from me and glanced around the room, a smile formed on his lips.

'You can project.'

'What?'

'This, all this,' he gestured with his hands, 'Rosie, you're making me see what you want me to, that's projection.'

I stood up and walked around the room, if this really was just an illusion, I wanted to see how real it really seemed. Greyson and Caleb would still be in the room somewhere, oblivious to what me and Ezra were seeing. I walked over to my desk where a picture of Ezra and me sat in a pale wooden frame, our initials carved into the base. I picked it up gesturing to Ezra, who was now standing behind me.

'Do you remember this?' I asked him.

'I remember everything Rosie,' I could feel his breath against my neck.

'And this?' I lifted up a small silver charm bracelet with emerald and sapphire stones.

'I gave that to you on your sixteenth birthday,' he paused, 'emerald and sapphire are your two favourite gemstones.'

I nodded and traced my hands over the rest of the contents on my desk before stopping on a small handwritten note. Ezra's hand reached out and touched mine.

'You don't need to read that,' he said, sounding almost embarrassed.

'I think I remember this though, it was for my tenth birthday, right?' I turned my head to look at him, he was even closer than before and my heart was beating so fast I was afraid he would hear it.

'Yes,' he was definitely blushing now.

Rosie, you're my best friend and I hope we stay best friends forever. PS. Being grounded was worth it, sorry about your knee, hope it heals soon. Enjoy your party. Ezra.

'Ezra … I …'

He looked at me and clenched his jaw, he kept looking to me and then to my lips and I to his. Then all of a sudden, the lights switched on and we were standing by a sink with the hospital bed in the room again. I blushed, remembering Greyson and Caleb were here and Greyson looked irritated. Caleb on the other hand had a grin plastered across his face that couldn't be any more obvious.

We called it a day after that and went off to our rooms. Ezra slept on the sofa and gave Greyson his room with Caleb. I was glad he stayed in our suite instead of requesting another.

Chapter 12

The next few days continued much the same, Greyson insisted on coming along to my training every evening and Caleb would sometimes join us. Grey had started training with Caleb and he was doing well in spite of having the disadvantage of being human. Grey and I still hadn't had the talk he had asked for when he arrived almost a week ago and we were in this weird limbo with our relationship. Neither of us quite knowing where the other stood. We would act like a couple one minute and be distant with each other the next.

My abilities were improving, though I still needed to speak to Ezra. I had a suspicion I might have more than just one additional ability, but I didn't want to talk about it in front of Greyson, which was getting near to impossible. Everywhere I went, Greyson followed, Ezra and I hadn't been alone since he had arrived. Ezra focused on helping me to hone my abilities more than the other aspects now, confident I was strong enough to fight in a battle against an enemy and capable of using a weapon without causing danger to myself. Thanks to his help I was expanding my projection and was now able to include Greyson and Caleb, showing them what I was seeing. I still needed help turning it off and on and choosing which scene I wanted to project. That part was proving difficult.

Greyson and Caleb were sparring on the mats as I practised my shooting next to Heather. I felt my heart pick up pace and turned around knowing who I was about to see. Ezra. He was walking around the gym and getting stopped as usual by people asking for help and advice. I think that was part of the reason he wanted us to train in privacy. It wasn't long before he reached me, standing behind me and placing his hand gently on my back, I sucked in a deep breath at his touch that sent light shivers throughout my body. His touch was so unique to me, he was standing extremely close and lowered his voice inching closer so only I could hear him. 'Let's train now', I turned around to face him, our bodies now touching, his hand resting gently on my waist.

'Now, in front of everyone?' I said. I knew I had gotten better, but I was afraid to practise in front of everyone. I liked the bubble we had created here at night without extra eyes on us. Then there was the fear, what if I failed and made a fool of myself yet again?

'You're ready Rosie, we don't need to keep training behind closed doors anymore', he smiled.

His words saddened me, I liked training with him in the evenings. I had grown so used to it, and the thought of not getting some time alone with him anymore wasn't something I looked forward to. As if he could read my mind he spoke again. 'We will still meet the same for the next week or so. It's just you need to practise your projection, and what better than on a room full of people? If you can make them see what you want, we could really use that to our advantage against Xavier.'

I nodded and smiled, now feeling better that we would still be seeing each other tonight. I realised then that we were still in the same close embrace and a few eyes were on us, most noticeably, Greyson's. Ezra stepped away and took a few steps forward before speaking.

'Ok, listen up! Rosie's going to try something new with her ability, so I need all of your attention. Just let us know if you start seeing a different surrounding than the gym, ok?' Everyone had stopped what they had been doing as soon as Ezra opened his mouth. Kai might have been in charge, but you wouldn't know it when it came to the respect Ezra had earned amongst our people. He was a born leader.

Everyone gathered around us, including Greyson and Caleb. This was the first time anyone outside of the four of us was told about my ability and I felt nervous. All eyes were on me. Ezra gestured for me to move into the centre of the now very overwhelming crowd. I stood beside him as he pulled me toward him, we were standing face to face with our eyes locked on one another.

'Just focus on me Rosie.' He took my hands in his and met my gaze. It worked, it was like I had completely forgotten our audience and it was just the two of us.

'Breathe,' he said softly.

I inhaled deeply and exhaled letting out an audible breath.

'Now close your eyes and imagine what you want to project.'

I closed my eyes and immediately the image of our beach on Atheria entered my mind. A memory with Ezra. We were sixteen and had just started dating, we snuck out of our homes together and had gone to the beach. It was breathtakingly beautiful and it's where we shared our first kiss. The beaches back home were different to the ones on Earth, the sand a pale, almost powder blue and the ocean matched the sky which showed colours of purple, blue and specks of gold mixed together perfectly. As the water rippled it reflected the colours in different intensities. Darkness never fell on Atheria the way it does on Earth, the closest description would be like a late summer's night where the sky has dimmed but the sun still shines, with the moon visible. That's what it's like back home, that beautiful coloured sky, it was one of my favourite places to go and I missed it.

'I see it!' Heather screeched.

'Me too,' Caleb said.

'And me!' Greyson exclaimed.

Relief fell over me, I had included at least one more person in my sight.

Then just as Heather, Caleb, and Greyson acknowledged my vision, more and more familiar and unknown voices acknowledged it too. I opened my eyes to see our group of thirty or so standing on a beach in Atheria. I looked at Ezra his smile stretched across his face. I wondered if he'd known which memory I had used to project.

People started to run toward the water and got even more excited when the splashes they made caused their clothing to become wet. I wanted to hold this image forever, I missed home so much it ached in me. Seeing these projections brought everything back and I wondered if the beach was still intact, or if the war had damaged it somehow. I felt a sudden rush of tiredness wash over me, making me feel weak, it must have been projecting to so many additional people. But I wasn't about to release the image yet, everyone was so happy. Ezra glanced at me and wrapped his arms around me, holding me up as my legs started to give way. It was taking every bit of energy I had to keep the projection alive.

'That's enough now, you can stop.' Ezra sounded worried.

'No Rosie, just a few more minutes.' I heard an unfamiliar voice exclaim and Ezra glared in their direction.

'Rosie, look at me,' he pulled my chin up to face him. 'Stop. Please, you're hurting yourself.'

'But they are so happy.'

'And they'll be happy again when we are really standing on that beach, once we win this war. But you exhausting yourself isn't going to help.'

I sighed and reluctantly released my vision, bringing us back to the cold training gym, a far cry from where we just were. My legs completely gave way and Ezra scooped me up into his arms, carrying me up the twisted staircase to our suite, without so much as a word to anyone else. He laid me down on the bed and I sat up leaning on my elbows to look at him.

'I'm fine. Really, I just didn't want to leave that moment.'

'Do you rememb—' he started but stopped. 'That was amazing, and it worked, but you need to pace yourself all the same. The time you can withstand it will get longer the more you practise, but you can't let yourself get hurt trying to please everyone else. It doesn't matter what they want, you need to look after yourself first.'

'Of course it matters. They are our people, the same people our parents lost their lives for, so if I can make them happy even just for a moment, I will. I know what you're saying, and I'll be more careful I promise, but I just couldn't let go today.'

He sat down beside me on the edge of the bed and studied my face, a small smile tugging at his lips as he shook his head.

I looked down and smiled, 'And yes, I do remember. I remember that night very well. Why do you think I pictured that scene?'

He grinned, moving closer to me and raised his hand, tucking my hair behind my ear. He rested his hand there as I closed my eyes, leaning into the warmth of his touch. We heard the door hinge unlock and Ezra let his hand fall back to his side. I instantly missed his touch.

'Rosie, are you ok?' Greyson entered into the room with his brows furrowed, looking concerned as he made his way toward me. I watched as Ezra stood up, passing Greyson without another word.

Chapter 13

I fell asleep not long after Greyson left my room and slept until the next morning. I wasted a whole day and night because I had exhausted myself so much. Ezra was right, I was going to have to slow down before I tried anything like that again. I woke up absolutely starving and got dressed as quick as I could so I could make it to the main hall in time for breakfast. I only had ten minutes left so I knew I wasn't going to be left with much choice. I closed my bedroom door behind me and entered into the living area, Ezra, Caleb, and Greyson were sitting between the sofa and the armchair, they seemed deep in conversation. I was glad all three of them were somewhat getting along. As my eyes scanned the room my gaze came to a stop when I reached the dining table. It was covered in the same food usually available downstairs. As I walked closer it was obvious it was for me. Everything there was what I would usually pick from the selection downstairs.

'Which one of you did this?' I said, interrupting their conversation. Greyson and Caleb hadn't noticed me enter by their reaction, although Ezra seemed to know I was there all along.

'Ezra.' Greyson said through slightly gritted teeth.

'Thank you so much, I'm starving.' I lifted the plate and started to fill it, the smell of everything already had my mouth watering.

'I thought you would be after yesterday,' he said, as a confident smirk pulled at his lips.

I took my plate and walked toward the sofa, taking a seat between Ezra and Caleb. Greyson occupied the armchair. Caleb stood up almost immediately as I sat down and walked toward the table, lifting a pre-filled breakfast bagel and taking a bite. Greyson took the opportunity to take the now empty space, sandwiching me between him and Ezra. I caught Caleb smirking at the gesture. Greyson then draped his arm over me, so I would be leaning closer to him. My body involuntarily shuddered at his touch. I had no idea why, it's not like Greyson repulsed me, he was still my boyfriend after all. I had never had that reaction to his touch before. He didn't seem to notice thankfully, as he grabbed the remote and started to flick through the channels. Though when I caught Ezra's eye, he was grinning watching me.

'I'm going down to the gym, anyone want to join me?' Caleb said, looking to us to see if there were any takers. If it wasn't for yesterday, I would have jumped at that opportunity, but I planned on resting until my usual training session tonight to give my body time to recover. Ezra took him up on his offer after a few moments of silence, and left through the main door with Caleb, glancing back at me still smirking as he left.

Greyson had settled on a documentary about world war two and I was onto my second helping of breakfast when he broke the silence between us. 'So, since you aren't training until tonight do you think we could go for a walk around the grounds and catch up?' he spoke while his eyes stayed focused on the documentary.

'Yeah sure, just let me get a shower first.'

He nodded and raised his feet onto the coffee table. I had no interest in watching anything to do with war considering we were heading into one in the very near future. Once I had finished eating, I grabbed a towel from the linen cupboard, and jumped into the shower. I stayed there under the heat of the water a little longer than I needed. I was nervous about the conversation Greyson would undoubtably want to have.

I opened my bedroom door to see Greyson standing waiting with his navy jacket zipped halfway up. I hesitantly stepped toward him as he put his hand in mine. We walked together out of the castle in silence, until we reached a small gravel pathway that circled the perimeter of the castle.

'I'm sorry,' he began, breaking the uncomfortable silence that had fallen between us.

'Why are you apologizing to me? It should be me apologizing to you,' I looked to him confused.

'I shouldn't have told you to leave.' Grey looked down to his feet with an ashamed expression.

'You were angry, and you had a right to be.'

'I didn't want you to leave, I was just angry and I didn't want to say something I'd regret, you know?' he shrugged.

'I know,' I nodded.

'I have some more questions, if you don't mind?' he dropped my hand as we continued walking along the white gravel path, the stones crunching beneath our footsteps. I was relieved that he'd released my hand from his grasp, and that made me feel guilty.

'Ok, ask me anything,' I said, a little apprehensive. The last conversation we had that involved questions hadn't ended too well, and that made me nervous for the outcome of this one.

'All those childhood memories you told me, and your dream of going to Europe with me, were those lies?' he looked at me, but his eyes were glazed over like he was thinking about something else.

This wasn't going to be a light conversation for a early morning walk, I guess it was long overdue though. 'No, they aren't lies exactly, they are from someone else's life, someone else's memories, dreams, ambitions. I'm from another planet Grey, so Europe was never on my to do list.' I tried lessening the impact of the realisation that I wasn't the person Greyson had fallen in love with.

'Those things you talked about with Ezra when you first

projected, they were real weren't they?' Grey's eyes locked on me now and I could see the hurt in them.

I looked down to my feet, pretending to concentrate on my footing, unable to look into his eyes. 'Yes, that was real. Any memory from my past that I've told you about, unless it happened in the last three years, didn't really happen to me.'

'I thought so,' he looked forward now, averting his eyes away from me again.

'What do you mean?'

'Since I've been here, I can see you're not the same Rosie you were all those weeks ago,' his voice changed when he said my name. It wasn't the usual way he had said it before. It felt colder, like he was trying to distance himself from me.

'How so?' I'm not sure why I probed on, maybe I was afraid that if we stopped talking, what I feared most would happen.

'The way your face gets all animated when you talk about a memory from your home. I've never seen you talk about something as passionately before, it makes sense now. You seem surer of yourself, stronger I guess,' he smiled reassuringly at me, and I was confused. I thought he was going in a different direction.

I smiled at him in response and nodded. I guess he was right, humans tend to be more doubtful of themselves, and I think I adopted that living here without my real memories. It's taken me to be here with Ezra, Caleb and the others for me to get that back.

'What is it like, where you're from?' he changed the subject and I welcomed it.

'It's perfect.' I paused to smile, 'It's similar to here, yet there are so many differences. Atheria is incredibly beautiful and before all of this it was a truly peaceful place. I really wouldn't want to live anywhere else.' I paused, smiling. I could talk about Atheria all day if he let me.

'You miss it then?'

'So incredibly much,' I looked down to the ground, trying to distract myself from getting upset. I wanted to go back so badly I almost willed this battle to start, so we could end it and return home.

'When this is all over, will you—' he stopped as though he was choosing his next words carefully, then took a breath and continued, 'will you stay here or go back to Atheria?'

'I guess that depends on a lot of things.'

'Like what?'

'Well, if we win or lose. If Atheria gets destroyed in this battle. There's a lot for me to consider, I guess it's not just a simple decision.'

'You said that you wouldn't want to live anywhere else?'

'No … I mean yes, but …' I took a breath, feeling the air fill my lungs and then let out an audible sigh. 'I don't have the answer to that one yet Grey,' I lied.

'Ok,' he knew.

'Next question,' I asked, hoping to move the conversation on.

'I only have one more question.' The friendly tone in his voice had now disappeared and was replaced with a seriousness.

'Go for it.' We had walked almost the entire trail and the castle was getting closer to us with each step we took.

'You're still in love with him, aren't you?'

I stopped walking and stood still. Grey walked on a few steps more before he realised I was no longer beside him. He closed the gap between us and faced me, waiting for an answer. Although I had expected this sooner or later it still took me aback. His expression caused my stomach to drop. I looked into his eyes and the usual glimmer that was there when he looked at me had faded. His eyes were a duller shade of brown now, no longer bright.

'Grey ... look I—' I stopped for a moment, deciding what to say.

He nodded as if I had already answered, 'I know you are.'

'I didn't say—'

'You don't have to say Rosie. I've known you for two years and you've been my girlfriend for one of those, and before that you were my friend. I know you. I know when I see you look at him. I know because you looked at me like that before this all happened.' He looked down, avoiding eye contact.

'I can't do this anymore Grey.'

The words escaped my lips, a thought I was thinking though I didn't think I could actually say them. But then it was out there floating between us and an uncomfortable silence wrapped around us.

Greyson looked up into my eyes, taking a step closer to me, we were almost touching. He swallowed and clenched his jaw. 'I know,' his words barely above a whisper.

Tears escaped my eyes, rolling down my cheeks

frantically, like they had been held in and were now fighting their way out. He pulled me into his chest and wrapped his arms around me. I followed his lead and wrapped my arms around his back, crying into his chest. Minutes passed and I couldn't stop, my heart was breaking, and he just held me there for as long as I needed him, never once breaking our embrace.

Chapter 14

A week passed since Greyson and I broke up, it surprised me, the sense of relief I felt. It was like this whole situation had been weighing me down and now I finally felt free. Well, as free as I could be sharing a suite with my ex-boyfriend, my kind of ex-boyfriend even though we never broke up, and my honorary brother. I could really use Libby right now to even out all the testosterone. Grey and I were on friendly terms, which was good considering we all needed to have each other's backs at a moment like this. Although I might have come to the final realisation that even though I loved Greyson, it wasn't the same love I felt for Ezra. Since my memories returned, my love for Greyson had started to fade. It was built on another person's memories. Grey knew that the girl he fell in love with was gone, yet still here somehow. I considered many times erasing his memory of me and letting him go on and live a normal life again without heartbreak and war. But I would never do that without his permission, and he had already said no. It was like our relationship had a timer set from the beginning and it was unfair on both of us to keep it going.

No one knew that we had broken up yet, but I could tell they could sense something was going on between us. Although we've spoken since, it's been very cordial. Friendly yes, but nowhere near our normal level of communication. It gathered some strange looks and raised eyebrows from Caleb. Even Ezra had looked at us strangely on a few occasions. Breakups are a strange thing and not something I will ever be eager to go through again. The swell of emotions, the relief, guilt, emptiness, longing, are at times overwhelming.

At least we all knew where we stood, and I was fully focused on my training. With everything aired out I could finally breathe. I woke up earlier than the boys, making my way to the breakfast hall to nab the best of the selection, then hurried to the training quarters to work some more on my ability. My projection was lasting longer, and I was getting stronger, no longer nearly fainting. I knew my limitations and I didn't push them. I realised just a few days ago that I could project to places I had never been. I projected to a cobbled street in Paris, one of the places Grey and I had talked about visiting. What Greyson said before we broke up had stuck in my head, and then just like my other projections it had appeared before me so real, I could touch, feel, smell everything. Paris didn't have the same appeal to me anymore, though from seeing it through my projection, it was definitely a beautiful city and I could see why couples flocked there each year. Atheria didn't have large cities and I preferred it that way, natural beauty for me always outshone manmade.

I was throwing some punches at a slightly worn punching bag, when Caleb walked in, whistling to himself. He was the first one down from the breakfast hall and it would only be another thirty or so minutes before the place was packed out. It seemed like every day we were getting more and more recruits.

'Good morning Rosie,' Caleb said cheerfully.

'What's got you in such a good mood?' I asked, curious.

'Oh, nothing. Just a certain favourite girl of mine is coming next week for the party.'

'Libby's coming, *here*?' I asked with excitement.

Caleb had a grin from ear to ear and an extra spring in his step. His emerald eyes glistened with content and his cheeks were slightly blushed.

'Yes, only for the party though, and then I'm sending her back. I want her far away from here before anything goes down.' Caleb said still smiling, though with his last few words his voice changed tone, sounding tense.

'Ahh, I can't wait to see her.' Libby was exactly who I needed, and I missed her like crazy.

'What party though Cal?' I looked to him confused.

'They have them every few months apparently, Kai isn't overly fussed from what I've heard but it's meant to bring everyone together.' He rolled his eyes at that last part.

'Party or no party I'm excited to see her.'

'Me too, it's been way too long,' he paused, 'you might not have noticed, but I've missed her,' he whispered as a smirk appeared on his lips.

I gasped dramatically. 'What? No way Cal! I would never have guessed!'

We laughed together then Caleb's face suddenly

changed any evidence of laughter had disappeared. 'Are you going to tell me what's going on with you and Grey?' he looked at me to gauge my reaction, although it was serious there was a light undertone to his voice, making me think he was being cautious not to pry too much.

'We broke up.'

'I figured as much, are you ok?'

'Y … Yes. It needed to happen, it wasn't fair on either of us.'

'You're right. It wasn't fair on the three of you.' He shot me a knowing look.

'Ezra has nothing to do with my breakup with Greyson,' I said sternly.

'If that helps you sleep at night Rosie,' he chuckled and turned, walking toward the weights.

I decided today to practise more with my projection, the gym had started to fill up with people. So, I took myself off to the small side room Ezra had taken me the first time I projected. I opened the door, peering around it, making sure the room was empty before stepping inside. I closed the door tight behind me and flicked the lock so no one would disturb my concentration.

I closed my eyes this time picturing Venice, another

of the places Grey and I had dreamt about visiting. Our plan was to interrail staying in hostels to keep the cost down. When I opened my eyes I was standing on a small red bricked bridge, looking out as a gondola swayed down the river beneath me. The water rippled as the oar pushed against it. I followed the path in front of me passing by some tourists on my way, the narrow cobblestoned street held an array of restaurants and coffee shops. The smells of brewing coffee and fresh pastries filled the air. I inhaled the scents and took another step forward when my projection came to a sudden stop. Loud knocking echoed around me pulling me out of my projection entirely. The knocking persisted as I made my way over to the door and flicked the lock to open, the door pushed forward missing me narrowly.

'Sorry!' A gruff voice boomed.

'Liam! You nearly knocked me out,' I laughed.

Liam began apologizing as he stepped over the threshold. 'What are you doing in here?' he asked, gesturing to the empty room. It was probably just as well Liam's knocking had interrupted me; I had been getting dangerously close to a wall.

'Just working on my projection.'

'How's it going?' he walked over to the medicine cupboard and lifted out a bandage.

'Better, much better. The only problem is I don't want to leave them.' I chuckled.

'If I could project to Atheria I wouldn't want to leave it either.' He took a seat on the bed in the centre of the room and started to unravel the white bandage using one hand.

'What are you doing with that?' I asked, raising an eyebrow.

'Turns out I'm not so good with knives,' he smirked. I looked at the bandage that he was struggling with in his left hand. It was only then I noticed the crimson red blood flowing from his right palm. I walked toward him and sat down beside him.

'Let me help.' I reached out my hand and took the bandage from him.

'Heather was complaining I was getting blood everywhere.' He rolled his eyes, 'I couldn't take it anymore.'

I stood up and walked back over to the medicine cabinet, lifting out some alcohol to clean his wound and sat back down beside him.

'Yeah, Heather can be ...'

'Annoying,' Liam added.

I started to laugh; he wasn't wrong. Out of everyone I had met, Heather definitely had a unique personality. Even Knox was easier to deal with and he had constant mood swings. I would never know what version of him we would get. Nora kept him grounded though, and they suited each other even though they were complete opposites. Nora's personality was bubbly and bright, and Knox, was grumpy, antisocial and even rude at times. Then there was the odd, very odd time he would be nice.

'This might sting a little,' I warned as I dabbed some alcohol from the glass bottle onto a small piece of rolled up cloth. 'You ready?' I looked up to him for his approval.

'Go for it.'

The cloth connected with his skin, as I was careful to be gentle wiping away the excess blood. The once white cloth was now stained a deep shade of red. Once I was happy the cut was clean, I set the cloth down behind me and reached for the bandage.

'Thanks for this Rosie,' Liam smiled.

'Anytime, you could have just asked Ezra though.'

He looked at me, 'I think he has more important things

than to heal me anytime I do something stupid.'

'He would have done it.' I kept my head down and my eyes focused on wrapping the bandage over itself until the ends met and I tied it off.

'And he probably would have laughed, it's not that big of a cut.'

I held up his hand to him showing off my work and laughed. 'Yes this makes you look much more manly.'

He looked at his hand twisting it round and examining it with a frown, 'you make a good point.'

'I can go get him now if you want so you don't have to wear that thing.' I stood ready to go look for him.

'No,' Liam grabbed my arm stopping me.

'What?' I turned to look at him, his cheeks were flushed, and he looked at me pleading.

'Ok, fine you can walk around with that wrapped around your wrist if that's what you really want,' I smiled at him.

'Thanks Rosie, it's just,' he cracked his knuckles as he pushed off the bed to stand beside me, 'I don't want him thinking I'm weak.'

He cared what Ezra thought of him, they really do put

him on a pedestal here. Though it's strange for me I don't think I'll ever look at Ezra like that, to me he'll always be the boy that would sneak me out of my house so we could play together long past curfew. The boy who I shared my first kiss with, the boy that lets me see beneath the mask. And the boy I first fell in love with.

'He wouldn't think you're weak Liam.'

He shrugged, 'At least Heather can stop yelling at you now,' I giggled changing the subject.

'I don't think she will ever stop yelling,' he let out a loud laugh, as his nerves from before seemed to disappear.

'No way, Heather's the least opinionated person I know,' I smirked.

'Do you ever hate me for asking you to join our table?' He raised his eyebrow.

'Every. Single. Day.' I burst out into laughter with Liam.

We left the room, still laughing as we walked from the gym and headed to the main hall for lunch. Liam moved onto his infamous impressions, mostly of Heather, as we walked down the long corridor leading to the dinner hall, our loud laughter earned us a few strange stares from strangers walking by. Liam had become a real friend and it was nice to have someone else to talk to, our friendship was exactly what I needed.

Chapter 15

When I woke it was still dark outside, I slipped out from under the warm bedcovers, intent on getting a glass of water and then returning to bed. I flinched as my feet touched the cold stone floor and rushed to grab a robe, wrapping it tightly to keep me warm from the brisk castle air.

I opened the bedroom door and peered into the living room. Ezra was still awake. He was sitting alone with his head bent down and shoulders tensed. I decided my water and sleep could wait and walked over to join him. I took a seat on the sofa beside him and left a good distance between us. Ezra raised his head from the papers he was holding to acknowledge me, he looked deep in thought.

'What's that?' I curiously nodded toward the papers.

'Kai thinks there's going to be an attack soon against our defenses, he thinks Xavier is going to try to weaken us.' He rubbed his hand along the back of his neck, then set the papers down on the coffee table in front of us. Letting out an audible breath he relaxed his arm over the edge of the sofa, turning his head and leaning in closer to me. 'I've been going over all our bases trying to figure out which one he'll attack first.'

'We have more bases?' I asked, surprised no one had mentioned it before.

'We have a few scattered around for protection. None are quite as large as here though, only a select few know.'

'Where are your thoughts then?' I reached out to the coffee table, lifting up the papers he had set down moments earlier, and inched closer to him. Flicking through the papers I could see some detail and then images of the other sites. They were definitely much smaller than the castle we inhabited. Mostly cabins, old warehouses and some were just campsites. They were scattered across the country, so choosing the wrong site to defend could be costly.

'I'm thinking here,' he lifted the third page from my grasp, our hands touching briefly at his movement. I looked at the image of a small warehouse similar to the one he had taken me to after my accident.

'It makes sense. Some of our best weapons are kept there,' he glanced over my features, settling on my eyes.

'Just briefly looking at them, I think you could be right. Did you tell Kai?'

'Yeah, and he thinks it's going to be here,' he lifted the fifth and last page from my hand, showing a small cabin in a secluded woodland area. He shook his head silently, disagreeing.

'What would Xavier achieve by attacking here though? There can't be any more than twenty of us in there. Surly he would want to make more of an impact, and destroying some of our weaponry would be a good start,' I said, confused.

'That was my point to Kai.'

'And he just dismissed it?'

He nodded. I hadn't noticed until now, but we had somehow moved closer together during our conversation. Our knees were now touching and I became all too aware of it.

'Kai can be, difficult, sometimes,' he said, his tone dry.

'Does he know you took these?' I lifted the papers and

dropped them onto the coffee table.

He shook his head, 'No, and he won't find out. I'll have them back on his desk first thing tomorrow morning.' He smirked.

'Don't you trust him?'

'Yes. I do, it's just ... these people Rosie, they're *our* people. Kai's been wrong before, I don't want to take another risk like that again.' He glanced down to his feet.

'You feel responsible for them.'

'Exactly, and if I lead them to the wrong place it'll be us that pay that price. I have to be sure we are defending the right place.' Concern was written all over his features.

I nodded, and turned my body toward his, 'Then why don't you explain that to Kai?'

'Like I said before, he can be difficult, he's the one in charge. If I pull rank over him it could upset a few too many people.'

'It's not like you to take orders from anyone.' When he didn't respond I continued, 'Why is Kai in charge anyway? Like you said, these are our people. You should be the one leading them.'

'Because he's the reason I'm here Rosie, he got me out of that ... that prison,' he paused, I could sense he was uneasy.

'He was leading the uprising against Xavier for almost a year on Earth, gathering as many of our people as possible to help restore our planet. Without him I wouldn't be here.'

'So, you feel like you owe him?' I concluded.

'Yes.' His jaw clenched.

'Why did he come back for you?' It seemed strange to me that Kai would risk getting caught, and either killed or imprisoned to save Ezra, he didn't even know him before all of this.

'He didn't. He came back for his wife, but they had already killed her.'

'Oh.'

Kai was a difficult man to figure out. I definitely wouldn't have thought he had a wife, or that she was now dead. I couldn't make my mind up whether I liked him or not. Sometimes he'd be pleasant when he stopped by the gym or in the corridors, other times he would be rude and ignorant. My undecided feelings for Kai didn't matter when it came to this though. He lost someone too, like so many of us.

'I know.' Ezra said, his blue eyes now piercing into mine.

'I had no idea.'

'Not many do, it's not something he likes to talk about.'

'I get that.' I meant it. I could understand why Kai would want to keep something so personal as losing his wife guarded. I had barely spoken to anyone about my parents since I learned of their deaths, I didn't want to open up. I wanted to be stronger than I felt.

'How about you? How are you coping?' He must of known by my expression I was thinking about them.

'I'm ok.' I tried to shrug it off. If I started talking to Ezra about them, I knew all the grief I had bottled up would spill out to the surface and I was afraid of it.

'It's ok to talk about them, and it's also ok if you don't want to. Just know I'm here and I'll listen, or I'll stay in silence with you if that's what you need.'

'Thank you.' I smiled at him, 'I'm just not ready to talk about them yet. But I will, I promise.'

'Ezra?' I whispered.

'What?' He tilted his head closer to hear me.

'What … What happened when you were a prisoner?' This question had been on my mind since my memories returned and I saw the scars on his hands and face. But I was too afraid to ask after what Caleb had told me, I wasn't sure

I was ready to hear it. His eyes glanced to our now touching knees and then to my face, his expression tore at my heart. I felt a sudden pang of guilt for asking him to open a wound to such a sensitive topic after I refused to do the same.

'Nothing good,' he clenched his jaw again and I watched as the muscles in his face retracted. He moved his hand that was now resting on the cushions behind us down to my waist, stroking me gently with his hand as if for comfort.

'You don't have to tell me.' I rushed to take back my question, regretting it the moment it slipped from my lips. Hearing his reply only made me regret it more.

'No it's not that Rosie,' he continued, 'it's not that I don't want to tell you, I just don't know how.'

'Then don't it's ok, I shouldn't have asked anyway.' I went to stand when he pulled me back.

'I'll show you,' he said, before releasing his hold on me.

'You really don't have to Ezra,' I protested. Though it was too late as he started to lift his black shirt up over his head, exposing his torso. I gasped when I saw his body. It was nothing like it used to be, where his skin was once smooth it was now jagged, silver and red scarring encompassed his body. Without thinking I lifted my hand and traced along each scar. They trailed to his neck, one that I had already been accustomed to seeing and the light silver scarring on his right cheek. I had no idea that those visible scars were just the beginning. The scars on his hands drifted along his arms, his back, his neck, all of the exposed skin he was showing me was now obscured and marked. When I reached the scarring over his heart his hand reached up to cover mine. I hadn't even realised tears started to escape from me, until Ezra reached his hand up to brush them away.

'It's ok Rosie, I'm ok now,' he said, comforting me.

I felt terrible he was the one comforting me, I was in so much shock over what he must have been through. Nothing could off prepared me for seeing him like that. He witnessed his parents being murdered and countless others, and he went through unimaginable torture as evidenced on his skin. I felt anger at whoever did this to him, how they could take someone so perfect and beautiful and distort him. Whoever did this was evil, there was no doubt in my mind and seeing him like this lit a fire in me, engulfing me in the flames. We would win this war. I was sure of it and every part of me believed it.

Chapter 16

I paced back and forth as I waited in Kai's office. I had marched down here first thing after my conversation with Ezra last night. There were a few things I needed to talk to him about and I knew if I didn't go early someone would stop me. I felt sorry for what Kai had been through but that didn't excuse his dismissal of Ezra. I paced the floor of his office, still thinking it odd there was no desk in the centre, only a small bookcase beside the door that I had missed on my first visit.

I walked over to the large windows and peered out at his view. Although Atheria surpasses Earth on its beauty there were still some sights that took my breath away, and this castle and the highlands surrounding it were one of them. His view was from the back of the building, showcasing the horizon against the treetops. I could see a few people already awake running along the path, a welcomed change of scenery from the training gym. I jumped a little as the large wooden door opened and then slammed closed. I turned around to find Kai standing still, watching me without saying a word.

'I need to talk to you,' I said sternly, standing up tall. It didn't sit well with me last night that Kai wouldn't listen to Ezra's concerns about the location of a possible attack. Ezra wasn't just strong and an excellent fighter. He was extremely intelligent and anyone to doubt that was in my mind an idiot.

'Rosie. What a pleasure.' Insincerity riddled his tone.

Even though Ezra had told me Kai's distressing past, there was something about this man that I didn't fully trust. I knew it was stupid, he was leading the uprising against Xavier. None of that could help me shake the feeling of unease I got when I was in his company. Kai gestured for me to sit, and I followed while he sat down next to me, positioning his body toward mine.

'What do you need to discuss with me?' he asked, his

tone seemed curious, but his expression was anything of the sort. He looked distracted, like he was thinking about something else.

I looked into his eyes and made sure not to break contact. 'The attack.'

He looked at me as surprise clouded his features. 'That's classified information,' he said dryly.

'I wasn't aware there were secrets kept from the leaders of Atheria,' I retorted. If he was pulling rank, then I would do the same. I didn't have the same loyalties to Kai as Ezra did.

He looked taken aback by my response. He probably expected me to be less outspoken like our first meeting.

'Yes, quite so. Ezra handles it. Let's keep it like that?'

I leaned in closer to him, my eyes glaring into his, 'No.'

'What did you say?' Kai's posture grew defensive.

'No Kai, I have a right to know, and Ezra had a right to tell me.'

'Oh, my apologies,' he said, his voice insincere again, 'I thought since you two are together he would handle the more intellectual side of these things. He has lived through it after all, while you've been, well, otherwise *entertained*.' He exaggerated the last word. I knew exactly what Kai was getting at and the more this man spoke the more he irritated me. When Ezra said he was difficult, he hadn't been lying.

'It doesn't take someone to live through a war to know how to fight it. When was the last time you were in the trenches Kai?'

He smirked. 'What did you come here to say Rosie? I have more important things that need my attention,' he said sharply.

'You're sending our men to the wrong place.'

'Ezra showed you the locations, didn't he?' his voice was rising, and he was starting to shed his cool exterior.

'Like you said yourself, Ezra has lived through it, not you, not me. He knows what he is talking about, *trust* him.'

'So, you let yourself into my office to ask me to listen to Ezra, does he always need you to speak for him?' he mocked.

'I think you know the answer to that Kai. Ezra is more than capable of speaking for himself. He knows more than you about this and is far more skilled than you in making an accurate decision.' If he was going to insult Ezra, then I would do the same to him. Ezra told me last night that Kai had made past mistakes when it came to important decisions and I figured it would be a sore spot.

'I think it's time you left and got back to your training.' His expression hardened as he stood up from his seat and gestured for me to leave.

'You're making a mistake Kai,' I said, trying one last attempt. He grunted, ignoring me. His arrogance infuriated me and I spoke again without thinking, 'wouldn't want to do that again, would you?' I couldn't help myself, the words just spilled out. Kai seemed to have that effect on me.

'I'll suggest this once to you Rosie. Keep your nose out of where it doesn't belong.' The right side of his mouth twitched as he spoke with venom in his words. He was warning me.

'If it concerns those of us that will be sent out there onto the front lines by you, then it concerns me. We all have our lives on the line Kai.'

'And do you doubt that your life concerns me Rosie?'

'I've only just met you, it's a little early for me to judge that, don't you think?' I glared at him.

He grinned, looking down at me. 'This conversation is over. Good luck with your ability, hopefully you figure out what yours is soon, time is ticking.'

I opened my mouth to speak then paused as I processed

his last words, 'figure out your ability.' He must not know. Why wouldn't Ezra tell him? I left Kai's office without saying another word. I entered the gym and began my usual routine, only this time I was lost in thought. Ezra had always seemed so relaxed anytime he spoke about Kai and anything he had told me about him, or that I had seen myself, certainly didn't line up with my meeting with him today. He had said he could be difficult, but he was more so than that today, he was incensed. Maybe he had too large of an ego to let someone march into his office and tell him his mistake. But something about Ezra not telling Kai my ability just wouldn't leave my mind. It could help us win. It could disorientate the other side long enough for our men to attack, yet he had withheld that information from Kai, why?

I sat around the lunch table with Liam, Heather, Nora and Knox in front of me. Grey sat to my side and Caleb was beside him, leaving the seat to my left free. I shoveled the food onto my plate, it had been a long day already and I had skipped breakfast. I felt Ezra's presence before I turned to see him walking toward us. He reached the table and took the seat beside me without saying anything, he gave me a quick smile and started piling his plate nearly as high as mine. Heather and Nora noticeably stopped their conversation to stare at him. Knox didn't look up once, he was either reading something or concentrated on his food half the time anyway, and Liam was deep in conversation with the guy next to him but glanced over for a quick second before turning his attention back. This was the first time since I arrived that Ezra had sat with us and that didn't go unnoticed by the table.

'Here man,' Caleb leant behind us to pass Ezra a drink then continued talking with Greyson.

'So—,' he dropped his voice low so only I could hear him, turning his head toward mine. I had a full mouth so I nodded for him to continue.

'I heard you had a meeting with Kai,' he smiled.

'What?' I asked, surprised that Kai would want that conversation replayed to anyone.

He cocked his head slightly, peering his blue eyes into mine, 'You really riled him up.'

'Well he should have listened to you,' I spoke softly,

Heather and Nora still hadn't taken their eyes off him.

He laughed, 'Always having my back.'

'Always,' I said, laughing.

'So, did he change his mind?' I asked, now curious.

Ezra's laugh settled and he looked at me with a serious expression. 'No, he removed me from the team,' he shook his head, annoyed.

'He's an idiot.'

His smile came back and he leant closer to me, his hand raised up to brush a curl behind my ear, 'You don't like him, do you?' he whispered as he leaned in closer.

I rolled my eyes and shrugged, 'What's not to like?'

He leant his head back and started laughing again and this time it was louder, gaining a few more stares from those around us.

'Ezra?' I asked.

'Yes?'

'We're going to that warehouse, if you think that attack is tonight. I'm not risking Kai being wrong.' I wasn't going to risk lives because of Kai's ego.

He looked at me, but he already knew how serious I was, he knew me better than anyone.

'Ok,' he nodded in agreement.

We broke from our conversation, turning our attention back to our still very highly packed plates. Heather looked like she might have been drooling, and Nora had started talking to Knox. I knew we would have to be discreet so Kai wouldn't find out. That only left us with two other people we could bring, the only two people we could fully trust not to tell Kai.

Chapter 17

We waited until night had fallen, providing us with the perfect cover. I took a seat in the back of the jeep beside Greyson, and Caleb rode up front with Ezra driving. The boys had flipped a coin on who would drive, apparently my driving skills weren't good enough to be considered. You have one accident and they never let it go. Caleb reached for the radio as soon as the castle was out of sight, blaring a ridiculously upbeat pop song on the radio that really wasn't fitting for the situation at all, that was Caleb never taking life too seriously.

We had been driving for a while and listening to Caleb's awful playlist when we finally turned onto the narrow road that led to the warehouse. It was surrounded by the forest like so many of our bases. I guess the trees provide the perfect cover. Ezra pulled off-road, hiding his black jeep amongst the forest, it wouldn't be seen here. He switched off the engine and glanced at me in the rear-view mirror.

'Everyone clear on the plan?' Ezra turned in his seat, looking to all three of us.

We had ushered Caleb and Grey to our suite not long after lunch and devised a plan together. We were going to meet the leader of the base, who would hopefully be more welcoming than Kai. Though that wouldn't take much. Then we planned to take their weaponry and hide it in a different location, staking out in the forest to keep an eye on the perimeter. We had a walkie talkie with us for communication to the warehouse. If Xavier's men were coming here, it would be to destroy the weapons, so guarding them was our top priority.

'Yes,' we replied in unison.

'Good, let's go,' Ezra jumped out of the car, moving to my door and holding it open for me. Seeing this, Caleb decided to open Greyson's door for him. 'After you,' Caleb said to Grey in an overly dramatized voice, holding out his hand and bowing slightly. Greyson shook his head laughing as he nudged Caleb out of his way.

'What man? I didn't want you to feel left out,' Caleb said acting hurt while putting his hand over his heart and laughing.

We made our way to the boot of the jeep and picked our weapons. The warehouse looked like it was completely abandoned from the outside, the only thing that gave it away was a faint glimmer of light glistening on the small lake in front.

Ezra opened the large warehouse door, swinging it to one side and gestured for us to enter. He had never been here before, but you wouldn't have known it by his confident exterior.

'Ezra,' a loud gruff voice shouted.

'Caspian,' Ezra smiled.

The man behind the voice came into view. He was around the same age as Ezra, maybe even a year or two older. He was muscular with short dark black hair, olive skin, and hazel eyes. He was wearing combat style black trousers paired with a black short sleeved top, showcasing a large tattoo that trailed up his arm and disappeared under his sleeve. They greeted each other with a handshake-turned-hug.

'They let you be in charge up here?' Ezra said, joking.

Caspian laughed, 'Better me than you.' He looked beside Ezra, his eyes scanning over Caleb and then me and Greyson.

'You must be Rosie,' he said gesturing toward me and reaching out his hand.

'That's me,' I smiled, shaking his hand as he looked me over.

'I've heard a *lot* about you,' he said, smiling and gazing back to Ezra with a playful smirk.

'This is Caleb,' Ezra cut Caspian off, turning his attention toward someone else, and I was thankful.

'I've heard about you too, looks like you stick by your word,' he looked toward me again and I suddenly felt my cheeks redden. Caleb give him his menacing grin and nodded.

Caspian walked over to Greyson last, he looked at him like he hadn't even noticed he had been standing there the entire time. His expression had hardened instantly.

'You are—?'

'Greyson,' I spoke, not liking that the warm reception Caleb and I had got had suddenly disappeared when he got to Grey.

'Greyson,' Caspian repeated with a sly smirk.

Greyson gave him a genuine smile and moved a little

closer to me. Whether or not he had noticed Caspian's change in tone the way I had, I wasn't sure, but I felt like it was obvious enough. I guess now wasn't the time to start throwing punches when Xavier's men could be fast approaching.

'How do you two know each other?' I asked, trying to divert from the glare Caspian was now shooting at Greyson.

'We were both prisoners of war together,' he walked over, taking his original stance in front of Ezra. The word *prisoner* struck a chord with me, I felt my body stiffen and a shiver run down my spine.

'He took Caleb's place in the cell when he left, we kept in touch once I arrived here with Kai,' Ezra said, turning his head to look at me. He moved closer to me, our bodies inches away from touching.

'Didn't know this is where you were though,' Ezra said, as he motioned to the warehouse.

'You know Kai, he had me sworn to secrecy. I swear if I had told anyone he would've sent me back to that prison,' he laughed. I wouldn't put it past Kai though.

'So, I'm guessing you aren't here for a reunion?' Caspian crossed his arms.

'Kai thinks there's going to be an attack tonight.'

'I know that, he thinks it's one of the others though, not here?' he frowned.

'Exactly,' Ezra said.

'Ah, you think it's going to be here because of the weaponry?' Caspian concluded. 'So, what's the plan?' he rubbed his hands together, almost excited.

It shocked me a little how quickly Caspian got on board with Ezra's plan and his thoughts on the attack when only hours earlier Kai had taken him off the team for the same reasons. Although maybe if I hadn't spoken to Kai, he wouldn't have removed him, but that's beside the point. Caspian trusted Ezra and I could tell Ezra trusted him, just like with Caleb. I guess when you go through that with someone it bonds you to them in a way no one else could ever begin to understand. Ezra and Kai however did not have that same history, so it's understandable there's a lack of the same 'I'll jump if you jump' kind of trust. Well that, and he's just *difficult* as Ezra puts it.

Some time had now passed since we hid the weapons, only the five of us knew where they were moved to. Caspian didn't want anyone else knowing their location in case of an ambush. Xavier's men would likely torture anyone for information and the less they knew, the better. We were perched with our backs against the trees, taking cover. An hour or so had passed and so far, nothing. Then just as Caleb opened his mouth to start another conversation, we heard stones crunching. It was coming from the road. We turned our heads at the sound and Ezra radioed Caspian to prepare them. The footsteps were closer now and we could make out about ten of Xavier's men. We waited for Ezra's signal, raising our weapons to our chests. We watched as they walked directly to the small barn where the weapons had once been kept. They knew exactly where to find them without any hesitation and as I looked to Ezra, I could tell he was thinking the same as me. How did they know exactly where to go? When they realised the barn was empty the men marched back toward the gravel path and to the entrance of the warehouse. We moved swiftly, avoiding the pathway, so our footsteps were silent. We raised our weapons just as the door to the warehouse swung open and Caspian was standing with his men armed.

'Drop your weapons!' Caspian yelled.

My hands were shaking, this was the first time my training would be used and luckily for me, Caspian's men far outnumbered Xavier's. The men and some women dropped their weaponry to the floor, creating a loud thud.

'Get inside.' Ezra nudged one of the men with the barrel of his gun. The rest followed his instruction, immediately moving inside.

'Sit,' Caspian ordered.

They each collapsed into a row of chairs that had clearly been laid out for this exact reason. I lowered my gun slightly, not taking my eyes off the group of people now sitting in a line. As I looked at each of their faces, they looked no different to us at the castle. I don't know what I was expecting, of course they would look normal. But these people, they were trying to destroy worlds. My world in particular. I just couldn't grasp why you would ever fight for the wrong side.

'Listen up. This is how it's going to go. You answer my questions and you live. You don't answer my questions and you die. I won't repeat myself again.' Caspian's voice was harsh, and it scared me a little how his tone could be so cold. Although Caspian and Ezra were good friends, they clearly had opposing opinions of how to deal with prisoners of war. I didn't want to stay to watch Caspian pick them off one by one. I knew if they truly believed in Xavier's reasoning, they would die for him. Just like I would die to protect Atheria and the people I love.

Ezra had moved to stand beside me and lowered his voice, 'Caspian's got it from here, we should go.'

I nodded trying to brush off the knot that pulled in my stomach and wanting to get as far away from this place as possible. We walked out of the warehouse to the sound of gunshots, I didn't look back at those people once as I left. I knew I would never forget their faces or how scared they looked. This was my first experience of the effects of war and I had no doubt it would linger in my mind for the rest of my life.

Chapter 18

'Rosie!'

My eyes flew open as I heard a familiar high-pitched voice screech my name. I rushed to my feet swinging open the bedroom door and there beside the front door stood Caleb with a very excited Libby bouncing on her heels next to him. As soon as her eyes locked on me, she rushed to my side pulling me into a hug.

'Libby, you're here,' I said, smiling as I hugged her back.

'I've missed you so much Rosie,' she said as we broke away. She looked at me with a stern expression and grabbed hold of my arm, pulling me back into the bedroom.

'We need to talk,' her tone was nothing like Libby's usually bubbly voice. She was serious. How serious? I wasn't sure. Libby's scale of seriousness ranged anything from her dog dying to Caleb eating the last chocolate bar. So, it was difficult for me to judge.

'Libby, I thought you'd want breakfast,' Caleb spoke with desperation in his voice. He had just got her back and now she was distracted by me.

'Of course I do, but I need to talk to my best friend first,' she gave him a comforting smile. I liked that she still thought of me as her best friend even though most of our friendship wasn't real. I still thought of her like that too.

It was early. Really early, Greyson was in his room and Ezra was still asleep on the sofa until Libby had screamed at the top of her lungs of course. He had jumped about a foot off of the sofa. We were all on high alert after last night and Libby barging in screeching definitely didn't help matters. I glanced over to Ezra yawning and Caleb taking a seat beside him, reaching for the remote.

She hurried me into my room, closing the door with a thud and took a quick glance over her surroundings, nodding her head in approval as she sat down on my still messy bed, gesturing for me to sit beside her.

'Libby, this better be important, I still had another half an hour before I had to get up.' I yawned and stretched my arms.

She rolled her eyes dramatically at me. Libby had always been a morning person. I seriously had never met anyone so full of life the moment their eyes opened. She always purposefully woke at five in the morning. She said it made her more productive. I think it's because she enjoys life so much that sleep is an inconvenience to her. Whatever the reason, I wouldn't change her. Well, maybe I would change her for half an hour so I could sleep.

'What are you wearing to the party?' She couldn't even hide her excitement. That was it? That was what was so urgent. I fought back a chuckle. Of course, that was the most important thing on Libby's mind right now. It brought back memories of the parties we would attend, she always had us plan our outfits in advance. It was a nice change to have someone to talk to about simpler things like a party.

'I haven't thought about that yet,' I answered truthfully.

The last couple of days had been a blur and after the *almost* attack last night, an outfit for the party was the last thing on my mind. Kai had already been alerted by someone when we returned and he was livid at first, though his mood abruptly changed to thank us. After all, if it wasn't for Ezra, we would've lost so many of our weapons last night. Then there was the concern that Xavier's men knew exactly where to go to find our weaponry. Kai took this upon himself to personally look into, it could only lead to one plausible explanation. There was someone on the inside working for Xavier.

'We need to fix that,' she said smiling as she walked over toward my wardrobe. She pulled out a few dresses I brought with me and started rummaging through them.

'I don't even know if it's a dress up kind of party Libs.'

She rolled her eyes at me again. 'Have I taught you nothing? Every party is a dress up kind of party.'

I shook my head, about to lie down as a loud knock sounded into the room. 'Come in,' I groaned.

'Are you two coming down with us for breakfast?' Caleb entered the room. A smirk tugged at his lips as his eyes drifted over to Libby.

'Come on Rosie, get changed and let's go, I want to meet everyone.' Libby threw a pair of work out leggings and a dark grey t-shirt at me as she left the room with Caleb.

'This is Libby,' I motioned to Libby, introducing her to the group. Heather and Nora broke apart from whatever they were discussing and said hello to her. Knox was scowling over something the person beside him had said and Liam hadn't joined us yet. Greyson and Ezra were surprisingly sitting next to each other deep in conversation. It wasn't long before Libby joined in on Heather and Nora's conversation about the party and their dresses. Liam arrived, taking the seat beside me and reached over to grab some food.

'You didn't injure yourself again did you?' I asked him.

'One time Rosie,' he laughed, shaking his head, 'I missed my alarm.'

'You going to this thing tonight?' he nodded over to the girls that, from what I could hear, were now onto discussing hair.

'Unfortunately,' I rolled my eyes. 'You?'

'It's not all that bad, I thought you're meant to love these things, being a girl and all?'

'I could think of better ways to spend my time.'

'Like training?' he raised his eyebrow.

'Exactly,' I responded.

He shook his head grinning. 'You'd be fast asleep if you weren't at that party, don't lie.'

'Maybe. I thought you were meant to hate these things, being a guy and all.' I smirked.

'Don't tell them my secrets,' he dropped his voice.

'Why do you like it so much?' I asked as I reached for my cup.

'The desserts.' He smiled and shrugged like it was obvious.

'Tell me more, I'm interested now.' I motioned with my cup, signalling for him to continue.

'Well, they seem to have a lot of choc—'

'Stop telling Rosie about the desserts Liam, for goodness sake. You haven't stopped going on and on about them for days,' Heather interrupted.

'Why else would you want to go to a party?' He shrugged, giving me a quick wink before piling some more food on top of his already packed plate, he puts me to shame.

Heather paused for a moment, giving thought to her response. 'It's fun.'

'It's fun,' Liam repeated in an impressively accurate Heather voice.

I tried to hold back a laugh and failed, I clasped my hand over my mouth to stop my laughter getting too loud, Libby and Nora let out hushed chuckles from across the table. Liam and Heather always managed to entertain me with their constant bickering, you would almost mistake them for siblings.

The hours went by and it was nice to have Libby back. I took time to show her my projection and told her all about Atheria. I'm sure Caleb had already filled her in, though she seemed interested and kept asking more and more questions. Caleb probably hadn't gone as in-depth as she would have liked; Libby always has been one for the details, a true perfectionist. After a walk around the castle it was time for us to start getting ready.

Libby and I were applying our makeup whilst we chatted some more about our lives. It's a strange thing to have felt like you've known someone almost your whole life and then go back and hit the restart button. It was obvious Libby and I would have been friends even without the made-up memories. We chatted about her life and what she had been up to since we all left, my breakup with Greyson, what my relationship with Ezra was like before everything had happened. Libby seemed to make a point of not bringing up the war and to be honest I had talked so much about it recently I didn't want to discuss it either.

'And what's going on with you and Ezra?' Libby probed.

'What?'

She winked at me and giggled. 'You know what. I've watched you two all day. You're like magnets.'

'I have no idea what you're talking about Libs,' I said, laughing along with her.

'Girls, you ready?' Caleb's impatient voice sounded from outside the door. Libby had warned him that under no circumstances was he or any of the other boys to enter my room while we were getting ready. It made me laugh how she had been here only a few hours and was ordering them all around. She moved to the door as I took one last glance at myself, the dark red dress Libby had lent me was beautiful. It pulled in at my waist and came out ever so slightly at my hips, resting just below my knee. The v-neckline and cap sleeves were exactly my style. It was as if Libby had brought it along just for me, and I wouldn't put that past her. I let my long curly hair loose for the first time in what felt like forever and it was a welcomed change. Libby's dress was equally as beautiful, a simple black empire line dress that floated above her knee, she had accessorized with a colourful necklace and braided her auburn hair to one side.

I followed Libby into the main living area of our suite where the three boys stood waiting for us. My eyes immediately drifted to Ezra's as he smirked at me.

Caleb beamed a smile at Libby, 'Let's go.'

Libby linked her arm in mine as we followed the boys to the dining hall. The main hall of the castle had been completely transformed. Gone were the usual tables and chairs, it was only now seeing the hall somewhat empty that I could take in the sheer size of the room, it was massive. The chandelier's glistened in the light and the buzz of people filled the room as they danced and chatted with one another. Large tables spanned along the far-left corner underneath the windows with the array of food and desserts just as Liam had promised.

My trail of thought broke as I felt a hand press on my back and a warm body lean into me. 'Want to dance?' Ezra's deep voice was lowered to a whisper.

'Yes,' I smiled.

He took my hand as he led me onto the dancefloor, His blue eyes looked like a storm of grey in the light of the room. I placed my hands onto his shoulder as his slid from my waist to my back, his touch gentle as if he was scared he would break me.

'You look beautiful Rosie,' he whispered.

I smiled and shook my head at him, 'You don't look too bad either.' I gestured to his suit, it was as black as the midnight sky, paired with a long skinny tie that matched perfectly. Handsome doesn't even come close to describing him.

'It's been a long time since you've seen me in one of these,' he laughed.

'It's perfect.'

He moved in closer bridging what little gap there was between us until our bodies touched, his grip tightened around me as I followed his lead. He rested his head beside mine, his lips inches away from the curve of my neck. Our bodies relaxed together in the gentle sway of the music, and in that moment, I had never felt closer to him. We stayed in the comfortable silence that seemed to speak a thousand words between us, yet not even a whisper of a word escaped our lips. Song after song passed by with our bodies entwined together, it felt too delicate a moment to break away and I didn't want to ever be apart from him again.

'Him!'

Kai's voice broke through the noise of the party, ceasing all music. People stood frozen around the room watching as he marched with his two guards accompanying him. He stormed past us and I looked to Ezra, reading his face to see if he had any idea what was wrong. His expression held no answers, appearing as confused as I was. The only sliver of knowledge I could gather was he seemed to be headed in the direction of someone. Ezra and I pushed past a few people that were staring at the scene that was about to unfold in front of us. I let out a gasp when I realised who Kai was after, Liam.

'What's going on here?' Ezra spoke up from beside me.

'Take him outside.' Kai ordered his men before turning to face Ezra, 'I'll talk to you about this in private.' Kai's voice was stern.

His men where already marching away, when Ezra took my hand. I kept up with his pace as Caleb, Libby, Greyson and Knox followed close behind. Once we were out of the hall the doors slammed behind us.

'What are you doing Kai? Let him go!' I yelled.

He turned on his heel and strode toward me with a furious expression, his eyes were filled with aggression. Ezra stepped in front of me, putting himself between us.

'Move.' Kai snapped.

Caleb, Greyson and Knox, closed in beside us, their eyes staying fixated on Kai.

'No.' Ezra said firmly, clenching his jaw, I looked down to see that his fists had turned inwards, his entire body tensed.

'You need to control *her* more,' he pointed aggressively around Ezra to me.

I could sense Ezra's anger rising as his body tensed even more, I placed my hand on his arm to try to calm him down.

'You need to watch your mouth Kai,' Ezra snapped back.

'Always sticking her nose where it doesn't belong,' Kai retorted.

'That's my friend. Let him go now Kai,' I demanded, taking a step forward. Ezra held out his arm, stopping me from getting closer to Kai and keeping himself between us.

Kai kept his glare on Ezra then addressed me, 'This *friend*, is our traitor.'

I looked to Liam as he shouted, 'I didn't do anything Rosie! You know I would never—' one of the guards moved his body in front of Liam throwing a punch that connected to his ribs. He choked and gasped as he tried to get air back into his lungs.

'Let him go,' I screamed.

'You want me to let that,' he pointed at Liam who was clutching at his ribcage, 'traitor go?'

'He's not the traitor.' I yelled at him, and this time I felt Ezra's hand gently touch my arm to calm me.

'Oh, is that so? And I guess you know who the real traitor is?' he sneered.

'Prove it,' I shouted.

'*Excuse* me?' he took a step closer and Ezra nudged me back a step.

'Stay away from her Kai,' Ezra warned.

I glanced to Greyson and Caleb and they were equally as tense. Both focused on Ezra's every move.

Kai let out a sickening laugh, 'I'm in charge here. I don't have to prove anything to *you*,' he paused and turned to Ezra. 'I thought you'd be able to keep her in her place, unless you would rather I do it?'

'I'm warning you Kai.' Ezra's fists tightened.

'Gets under your skin doesn't it? She'll end up just like her parents if she doesn't learn to keep that mouth of hers shut.'

Kai had barely finished speaking when Ezra's fist connected with his face, causing a loud cracking sound to echo throughout the empty hallway. Caleb, Greyson and Knox jumped beside Ezra, now eyeing Kai's guards who stayed completely still holding Liam. Libby let out a loud gasp. Kai raised his head, blood trickling from his definitely now broken nose. He was smirking as he wiped the blood. 'She's got you wrapped round her finger. You know that feeling all too well, don't you *Greyson*?'

Ezra went to move closer to Kai as I pulled his arm to stop him, he turned his head to look at me.

'Don't,' I said.

'That's a good boy, listen to Rosie,' Kai taunted.

Ezra kept his eyes on me as I moved to stand beside him, he moved his arm resting it on my hip, his grasp was firm, protective.

'Where are you taking him?' Knox spoke up.

'That's none of your business Knox. I'm done with this now.' He said, still clutching at his nose as he stormed away. I took a step forward to protest, when I felt Ezra pull me back.

'Rosie,' Ezra said facing me.

'I can't just let him take Liam.'

'I'll get him tomorrow, don't worry,' he said reassuring me.

'But how? Kai's not just going to forgive you for that,' I frowned.

'Don't worry about how. I'll get Liam, and Kai knew better than to talk to you like that.'

After Ezra spoke to the boys, we ended up back inside the party, though all I could think about was Liam. There was no possible way he could be the traitor. None. In fact, if you lined up everyone in this room aside from Ezra, Caleb, Libby and Grey, Liam would be the least likely suspect. I left the party early and headed to my room, closing the door on the night. I rested on the edge of the bed and let out a sigh, tonight had not gone as planned.

Chapter 19

My hand lingered on the zipper of my dress, my fingers pinched ready to pull down, when I heard a soft knock. I twisted the handle pulling the door toward me, Ezra stood relaxed, as his arm rested against the door frame, a smile tugging at the corner of his mouth. I stepped aside and motioned for him to enter.

'I just wanted to check and see how you are, after everything tonight,' he walked past me, his eyes glancing over the room, before settling on me.

'I'll be better when we get Liam back tomorrow.'

'First thing tomorrow I promise, he'll be back bickering with Heather by breakfast.' He said, as he moved to leave.

'Ezra?'

I didn't want him to go just yet. Our night had been perfect until everything with Kai happened and I wasn't ready for it to be over. Not yet.

'I ... I just want to say thank you, for everything. Not just with Kai tonight, with Greyson too. Thank you for bringing him here, you didn't have to do that for me but I'm glad you did.' I took a few steps closer trying to bridge the gap between us.

'Kai deserved it,' he grinned, as he stepped toward me, 'and I will always have your best interests in mind. I just want you to be happy, even if that means having him here. I want you to know though, I'm not going to give up on us.' He placed his hands around my waist drawing me close until our bodies finally touched. My eyes drifted over his features. I wanted to look at him, to really look at him. I wanted the time that had come between us to be erased. My hands rested on his chest as I gripped the fabric of his shirt, I tightened my grasp before relaxing it, bringing my hand up and trailing my fingers along the scar on his neck, I bit my lip as my gaze settled on his eyes. He was watching me, silently. His hands moved from my waist to my neck, and I felt my pulse quicken at his movement. His touch. It felt like electricity coursing through my veins. A thousand memories sparked back to life.

'I can't stay away anymore.' His deep voice was low, and soothing as he whispered into my neck. He pulled my chin up, his eyebrows were tensed slightly. He kept one hand tight on my waist while his other drifted back to my neck lingering for a moment before resting on my cheek. I lent into the warmth, taking in a breath anticipating his next move, when his lips met mine, soft at first. Gentle. Like our first kiss all over again, like these years that had come between us were being washed away. As we grew comfortable with each other again, our kiss deepened in intensity. Need, want, desire, filled the room, I ran my fingers through his messy dark hair, as his hands tangled in mine. Through it all, through all the pain, the separation, the loss, we managed to find our way back and nothing else mattered anymore. It was just us.

'I love you Rosie.' Ezra pulled away, his lips still grazing mine.

'I love you.' I smiled before pressing my lips against his and continuing our kiss.

I moved to sit on the bed propping some cushions up behind me and patted the space beside me. He hesitated before removing his suit jack swinging it over the back of the little chair nestled in the corner. I moved giving him more room, as his arm swung around my shoulders I lay my head against his chest. I listened to his breathing as his chest rose and fell and played with the end of his black tie, twisting the fabric between my fingers. We talked about everything. Everything we had both kept from each other these last couple of months. We talked like we used to, as if no time had ever come between us. Ezra finally opened up about what he had been through and I about my parents, the grief I was feeling and had bottled up. I felt as if a weight had been lifted from my shoulders. We laughed together joking with one another as we talked about old memories of our parents and Atheria.

I traced my fingers over his right cheek along his scar and leant up placing a gentle kiss there. We stayed together all night until we eventually fell asleep in each other's arms.

I woke with his hand tracing my shoulder, waiting for me to wake. I turned and looked up into his eyes unable to hide my smile.

'Good morning,' he said before leaning in to kiss me.

A knock sounded from my door as Caleb's voice shouted, 'Rosie do you know where Ezra is…?'

We pulled apart from our kiss as Ezra shouted, 'Come in.'

The door pushed open as a confused Caleb made his way in looking at us both before he smiled. 'Kai wants to speak to you Ezra.'

'What about?' Ezra questioned as he sat up.

'Don't know man, Alena left a note saying it was urgent. Probably something to do with last night.'

Ezra nodded and rubbed the back of his neck. He turned looking over his shoulder to me and smirked.

'So, you coming?' Caleb probed.

'Sure, I'll be out in a minute.' Caleb took the hint and left closing the door tightly behind him.

'I better get going, as much as I'd like to stay here with you,' Ezra leaned down and kissed me again, before retrieving his suit jacket. He flung it up over his shoulder and turned to me.

'I'll see you in the gym later?' I asked.

'I'll meet you there,' he grinned at me placing a gentle kiss on my head and left to follow Caleb.

I stood and picked out some clothing for the training gym, tying my hair back in its now usual slightly messy ponytail. I glanced at the clock I still had fifteen minutes before breakfast was over. I made my way to the fridges in the dining hall, grabbing a croissant and an iced coffee. I was halfway down the corridor when Greyson's voice sounded from behind me.

'Wait up,' Greyson yelled, as he ran to catch up with me.

'I'll come with you.' I nodded taking a bite of my croissant, we walked together down the rest of the corridor, across the courtyard, and to the stone staircase that led to the training gym. We stayed in silence until we reached the top of the stairs.

'Is Kai always like that?' he asked curiously, taking a sip of his coffee.

'He's never been that rude before, I'm not sure what has him so on edge, he was out of line.' Kai had really got under my skin last night, there was no doubt in my mind that he didn't like me. Not that it mattered to me either way,

I hadn't particularly liked him before last night, and now after what he said I was certain I would never like him.

'Are you ok?' Greyson now looked concerned.

'I'm fine,' I reassured him.

He gave me a look indicating he knew better than to believe my terrible lie.

'Really I am.' I insisted.

'You never could lie to save your life Rosie.' He laughed.

I rolled my eyes, 'fine, he annoyed me, but Liam will be released today and I'll get over it.'

'See was that hard?'

I glared at him, 'I think we should start with hand to hand combat?' I held back a laugh.

He spat out his coffee as he laughed, 'so you can kill me for making you tell me the truth?'

I winked as I stepped onto the mat, 'you're not scared, are you?' I raised my eyebrows.

'Course not.' He swallowed as he stepped up next to me.

'Just you know go easy, I am human you know.'

'You are?' I pretended to be shocked.

We started sparring as I kept one eye on the door waiting for Ezra and Caleb to return, intrigued by their meeting with Kai. I half expected them to come back and tell us we were kicked out of the uprising because of last night. I just hoped Ezra could convince Kai to let Liam go, otherwise we would be breaking him out of wherever Kai had him. Either way Liam would be free today.

Chapter 20
- Ezra -

'So?' Caleb started as soon as we left the suite.

'What?'

'You know what man, you and Rosie?'

I grinned and shook my head, 'What about me and Rosie?'

He laughed, 'Are you two back together?'

'I'm not saying anything.'

He looked at me knowingly and parted his lips to continue when I interrupted, 'Where's Libby?'

'She left first thing this morning, I didn't want her staying any longer not after last night,' he continued, 'what's the plan?'

'What do you mean?'

'For Kai and Liam?'

'If Kai doesn't let him go after we speak to him then I'm going to the basement to get him.'

'Count me in man. What was wrong with Kai last night anyway?'

I let out a breath, 'I have no idea, I'm getting fed up with his attitude though.'

'You and me both man, he seems to have it in for Rosie doesn't he?'

I looked at him and clenched my jaw, 'He was out of line, he forgets who she is.'

'And who you are,' Caleb voice was firm, 'you two will be leading us when this is all over, if you ask me you should be leading us now and not that—'

'I know.' I stopped him before he had a chance to finish and continued, 'he better have some apology for the way he spoke to Rosie.' I hadn't always seen eye to eye with Kai in the past and he had a tendency not to listen to me, but I had never seen him get aggressive until last night, and it didn't sit well with me that his anger had been directed at Rosie. He'd gone too far talking about her parents and taking Liam out in the middle of a party without any evidence. I'm as sure as Rosie that he is not the traitor.

'Well this is going to be fun,' he laughed.

I nodded to Kai's two guards Jared and Micah, as I pushed open the door without knocking.

'Ah Ezra, so nice to see you again,' Kai grinned as he greeted us. Was he serious? Caleb coughed loudly behind me, attracting Kai's attention.

'Caleb,' Kai looked him up and down.

'It's good to see how well you have been doing in training,' Caleb nodded briefly appreciating Kai's compliment, before his face contorted back to a frown.

'I need to talk to you both about something very important,' he moved his hand and gestured for us to sit. I had no intention of sitting and talking, he had a lot of explaining to do, this wasn't going to be one of our usual conversations.

'If this isn't an apology, I don't want to hear it.'

'An apology?' He questioned.

'Do you need a definition?' Caleb interjected.

'What for exactly?' Kai frowned, ignoring Caleb.

'Last night,' I clenched my jaw. I was starting to get fed

up with Kai. He wasn't stupid, he knew what he did last night, and he was skirting his way around it.

'Ahh right. Well, I'm guessing you aren't going to drop the subject, so fine, I'm sorry,' he gave the most insincere apology I think I've ever heard.

'That's not all Kai. If you ever speak to Rosie like that again you won't be in charge here anymore.' I hadn't noticed my fists had clenched until I caught Kai glancing down.

'Pulling rank now, and here I thought you were above that, Ezra,' he spat back.

I'd had enough of him. I was starting to question more and more why he was in charge. I knew if my parents were here, they would be leading, and I knew that's what they would expect from me. Kai had proven he wasn't always the best at leading the uprising, especially with the few times he sent us to the wrong location. I had a feeling Rosie was starting to question Kai's leadership capabilities just as much as I was.

'I'm above it, so much as you aren't stepping out of line with Rosie.'

'I see. *Always* about Rosie now isn't it? I'll agree to drop it.'

'And Liam?' I asked, hoping Kai would release him and

give up whatever ridiculous reasoning he had to arrest him in the first place. It would certainly save me some hassle later.

'Liam can be released. I know you would have released him today anyway, so there was no point.' We were right, he had no evidence that Liam was the traitor.

'Why did you take him if you knew he wasn't the traitor?' It didn't make sense to me that Kai would imprison Liam if part of him didn't think he was the traitor.

'I wanted to try and draw the real traitor out,' Kai said with a matter of fact tone. Something about that didn't add up for me.

'You're wondering why I was so harsh with Rosie last night aren't you?' he spoke like he was reading my mind.

'Yes,' I responded.

'She could have blown my entire plan. Liam isn't even in a cell right now, it had to look believable.' Kai had clearly given thought to his answer and the strange thing was I wasn't sure if I should believe him. He clearly didn't like Rosie. It didn't exactly take much for him to show aggression toward her last night and I didn't like it.

'Why did you ask us here Kai?' I was growing tired of our conversation.

'There has been an attack from Xavier at a base about an hour's drive from here. We need a small team to go and assist them in case of a second attack, it will take a few days.'

'Do you want me to suggest men?' I asked.

'No. I would like you, Caleb, and Greyson to go. I think you three will have this one under control after last time,' Kai responded with a smirk.

I questioned him, 'Are you sure we shouldn't take more men with us?' I was apprehensive that me, Caleb and Greyson would be enough to fend off an attack from Xavier's men.

'Please, you are being much too modest Ezra; I have heard just how far your team has come in the past few months of training. A second attack is unlikely, they really just need assistance, I want you there by tonight,' Kai responded dryly. His patience thinning.

'I just think that—'

'This is an order Ezra!' Kai replied, cutting me off.

'Maybe you should listen to your best soldier Kai, instead of ordering him to do a job that he doesn't think we're capable of.' Caleb cut in sounding defensive.

'With all due respect Caleb, you are under my command, so I will decide where I send you, and Ezra is fully aware of how I work here. I will not remind you again who is in charge.' Kai turned to speak directly to me, ignoring Caleb. 'I suggest you complete this quickly and remind your friend here to keep his mouth shut.'

'You—'

'I will let Grey know we will be leaving in an hour, but it might do you well to remember that although you are in charge, they are members of *my* team and I will keep them safe at all costs.' I abruptly interrupted Caleb. I wasn't done with Kai just yet but now wasn't the time. If there was an attack on one of our bases, they would need help and I couldn't risk people's lives over my growing want to put Kai in his place again.

'Yes. Good. You may leave now,' Kai said, gesturing to the door. I grabbed Caleb by his shoulder dragging him away from Kai.

We walked in silence until we got out of ear shot from Jared and Micah.

'I can't stand him,' Caleb said.

'I know, neither can I,' I agreed.

'I don't trust him Ezra,' Caleb looked at me worried.

'I may not like him for obvious reasons, but he has

never given me a reason not to trust him.' I tried to reassure him. It was true Kai had never given me any inclination that I couldn't trust him. Though as I said those words to Caleb, I started to doubt how much truth they held. Could I really trust Kai? Seeing him last night, the way he had been with Rosie showed an entirely different side to him, one I had never encountered before.

'Yeah well, we'd better go tell Grey to pack his bags,' Caleb picked up his pace clearly still annoyed.

As we entered the gym, I could already feel her presence as my eyes scanned the room for her. I walked over to the sparring mats and my eyes met hers. She was with Greyson engaged in hand to hand combat and she was definitely going easy on him. I smirked watching her, she had come so far in just a few months, it was impressive not that I doubted her for a moment. Rosie always was a quick learner. She was only a move away from flooring him, I looked down to check her footing, perfect. She blocked his arm countering his attack, as he took a step forward, a mistake that would lose him this match. Her eyes glanced down as she smirked and it was written all over her face, she knew. I waited expecting her to throw the final punch but instead she backed away, missing her opportunity and giving Greyson another chance.

'Time to pack your bags Grey,' Caleb spoke with a harsh tone to his voice.

They both stopped and looked directly at Caleb, Rosie smiled when she noticed me before her face hardened to a frown when she took in Caleb's words.

'What's with the tone Caleb? And what do you mean pack his bags?' She spoke.

I moved to stand beside her and placed my arm across her waist, kissing her gently on her forehead and leaning my neck down slightly to whisper into her ear, 'You shouldn't have asked.' I laughed as I warned her.

'Kai thinks he can just order everyone around now!' Caleb huffed before continuing, 'He's sending the three of us on a mission to help one of our bases that's been attacked.' I couldn't blame him for being annoyed. Kai wasn't doing much to be liked at the moment by any of us.

'How long are you leaving for?' Rosie asked, her hands gripped tightly around the back of my shirt.

'For as long as His Majesty wants,' Caleb hissed.

I grinned, 'Just a few days. So Greyson, we are best getting our stuff together now.' I looked over to Greyson who already had his eyes firmly fixated on us. He nodded in response. He wasn't all bad, I had talked to him a few times and we got along more than I'd care to admit. Rosie always had been a good judge of character. I wasn't sure if she had got the chance to tell him about us yet, but based on the look on his face she hadn't. He was watching my every move with her and I could sense she had noticed now too. She didn't let go of her hold on me though, I was glad. I didn't want her to.

Caleb started to walk out of the gym toward our suite as the three of us followed him. Rosie wrapped her hand around mine, squeezing as we walked. I squeezed her hand back and smiled as she returned the gesture again. A code we had from childhood.

'We'll be back in a few days,' I said as I threw the bags into the boot of my jeep.

'If Kai commands it,' Caleb muttered.

I looked over my shoulder to Rosie and rolled my eyes, her shoulders shook in laughter as she spoke to Caleb, 'I'll see you in a few days,' she said to him with a playful smirk.

She leant up to kiss me, pressing her lips to mine. I was going to miss her for the next few days.

'I love you,' she whispered.

'I love you too,' I was careful to keep my voice low. I could tell she didn't want Greyson to overhear and I understood.

'Come on Ezra, let's get this over with,' Caleb sighed. Rosie gave Caleb and Greyson parting hugs and moved to the steps of the castle to wave us off. I glanced back in the rear-view mirror at her before she drifted out of view.

Chapter 21

- Ezra -

I drove for an hour before we reached our destination. Caleb managed to talk from when we left the castle until we arrived, flicking through his playlist as usual. I parked close to the base, far enough away that my jeep wouldn't be seen, I wanted to be cautious in case of another attack. I smelt smoke in the air as I stepped outside of the jeep, there were too many trees to see where it was coming from.

'Something doesn't feel right about this.' Caleb opened the boot, choosing his weapon.

'I agree.' Greyson lifted out a gun.

'We'll scope the area, if something isn't right well go back to the castle and get a larger team ok?'

They nodded as I closed the boot, tucking the keys into my pocket. We made our way through the forest to the base. Harrowing screams roared in desperation as I stepped between lifeless bodies. The smell of charred flesh lingered in the air causing me to choke. I covered my nose with the sleeve of my shirt, keeping my gun tight to my chest, my finger hovered over the trigger. Ashes lay scattered across the floor as flames flickered through the building that was once the base. This attack had been far worse than Kai told us. Another reason added to the growing list why he was no longer fit to lead. I looked over each body trying to find any sign of life before my eyes locked on the source of the wailing. I stopped and signalled to Caleb and Greyson to follow. A middle-aged woman lay with a large piece of rubble covering her lower body. I could tell instantly she was not going to make it. Caleb and Greyson secured the area as I knelt beside the woman. Relief washed over her face, she reached out her shaking hand to me, I took her hand in mine. As I looked over the woman, I realized I recognized her.

'Eleanor?' I spoke low bending my neck down so she could hear me.

'Ezra,' her hand moved from mine to my cheek as she smiled before she started to cough. I placed my arm around her back and propped her up, helping her get air back into her lungs.

'I ... I'm not going to make it am I?' she said, struggling to speak.

I took her hand and closed my eyes trying to concentrate. I could feel her pain as it drifted into my body, I winced at the initial impact. The sound of her coughing forced my eyes to open and my concentration faltered. She was coughing up blood, I held her head up. 'Don't Ezra, it's too late.' She grabbed onto my arm squeezing.

'No Eleanor I can heal you,' I moved my hand back to hers closing my eyes again as she tugged her hand away.

'What are you doing?'

'Ezra. We don't have much time,' her coughing persisted. I looked at her in disbelief. She reached her trembling hand up to a golden chain that was hanging around her neck, tugged on it gently until it came loose and placed it in my hand. I looked down to see two stones, one an emerald and the other a sapphire, they were both entwined together and attached to a long chain with delicate golden leaves binding the stones together. I remembered this necklace as Rosie's mother had once gifted it to mine. It was meant to represent the two founding families and my mother had rarely taken it off. How did Eleanor come to possess it?

'It will open when you hold it. You ... you must keep Rosie safe,' she said taking a painful breath.

I could feel my heart thudding against my chest as she mentioned Rosie's name – something wasn't right.

'Who did this? Who attacked you?' I asked, hoping she would have the strength left.

'It's *him*,' she said with her final breath.

'Go! Now!'

I heard Greyson yell at me, he dragged me up by my shoulder forcing me to my feet. It was an attack, an attack on us. We lodged ourselves behind a car, shooting at a group of unidentified people. I looked over to Eleanor's lifeless body and noticed the gold chain lying on the ground next to her. I dropped it.

'Caleb, Greyson, I need to go back out there, can you cover me?'

'No Ezra, it's too dangerous. We don't know how many of them there are,' Caleb shouted.

'Caleb, I need you to cover me,' I said sternly to him. I needed them to cover me otherwise I wouldn't make it back alive.

'We've got your back,' Greyson responded, resting his hand on my shoulder, 'Go now.'

I ran quickly keeping low and grabbed the chain. They managed to shield me until I reached the safety of the car.

'We need a plan,' Greyson said.

'They're after us, they won't stop until we are dead,' I replied. More shots fired in our direction, we ducked and weaved from the bullets, our ammo was almost out. The jeep. It wasn't far from us. We just needed a distraction. I looked around trying to find something that we could use.

'Give me that bottle Caleb,' I pointed to the crate of glass bottles that were scattered along the ground beside him. I poured the liquid out and used the running petrol cascading from the car we were using as cover to fill the bottle. I ripped the bottom of my shirt, rolling it up so it would fit inside the bottle and used the fire beside us to light it.

'Shoot at them on my call and run for the jeep, don't stop for anything, do you hear me?' I threw the keys at Greyson.

'Yes,' they both responded.

'Now!' I yelled and threw the lit bottle into the centre of the car. We ran through the forest as fast as we could and made it to the jeep. The explosion provided the perfect cover for us to escape. Greyson wasted no time starting the engine, keeping the lights out he put his foot down and drove the car swiftly away from the base.

'Where are we going?' he asked.

'To the castle, something's not right about this, we need to get Rosie.'

'Agreed,' Greyson replied.

'What's with the necklace?' Caleb asked his eyes examining the chain wrapped around my neck.

I pulled the necklace off and took it in my hands just as Eleanor had said, sure enough it opened. A hologram appeared. Pages of my mother's handwriting, containing what looked to be confidential information. I flicked through the pages, taking in as much as I could. She wrote about the abilities passed down through the founding families. I read something briefly about an ancient bond between the founding families, Rosie and me. My stomach dropped when I flicked to a photo on the last page and read what my mother had inscribed beneath it.

'Drive faster!' I yelled at Greyson.

'I'm going as fast as I can, calm down.' Calm down Greyson said, how could I calm down? We needed to get back to the castle, back to Rosie. Now.

Caleb pulled the necklace from me. He began to examine the photo I had left on view. His face froze when he read the inscription, he looked up at me and swallowed. 'Drive faster Grey!' Caleb yelled.

'You two really need to stop yelling at me and tell me what's going on!'

'Rosie. We need to get to Rosie, she's … she's in danger,' I felt the colour drain from my face, and a sick unsettling feeling in the pit of my stomach.

Without asking another question Greyson pushed his foot down harder on the accelerator. If I could agree with him on anything, it was Rosie's safety. It killed me that we were still over an hour away from her. I needed to know if she was ok. She has to be ok. If anything happens to her, I'll kill him.

Chapter 22

Ezra, Caleb and Greyson sped off into the night. As I turned, making my way back into the castle a large man I hadn't seen before with a horizontal scar smeared across his neck grabbed onto my arm tightly, causing me to flinch.

'What do you think you are doing?' I asked, trying to free my arm from his grasp, he didn't respond. Pushing me instead down a long corridor and then several flights of stairs.

'I can walk on my own you know,' I hissed at him. He tightened his grip around my arm. I had never been in this part of the castle before, the basement, and a room I had been advised not to visit. I glanced to the man and then down at the dimly lit stairwell waiting for us, this wasn't right. Without thinking I let out a scream for help. He pushed me hard against the stone wall, clasping his hand over my mouth.

'Shut up. You're lucky he wants you alive,' his breath was warm against my skin.

'What are you talking about?' I struggled against his hold.

Without answering he continued to drag me down the final flight of stairs, this time keeping my mouth covered with one hand while his other held my arms together in a tight twist behind my back. He hesitated for a moment before pushing me through an open doorway. My eyes moved around the dark room one single flickering light hung from the ceiling so dim it barely lit up anything. But it lit up enough. Enough for me to know this was not just any room. It was a torture chamber, just like the prison Ezra and Caleb had told me about. He tied my arms to a pole above my head, tying a cloth around my mouth to keep me from screaming. To my left was a single chair and a table filled with instruments that sent a shiver down my spine as my eyes traced over them. The concrete floor beneath my feet was stained red and it wouldn't take much guessing to figure out why. I was left hanging there until my arms had gone numb.

I didn't understand who in the castle would want to tie me up in a torture chamber. Surely this was just another training method. Yes. That's what it is, just training. I tried to comfort myself with those thoughts although I could not escape the knot in my stomach nor the uneasy feeling I had experienced since entering this room. My thoughts vanished at the sound of heavy footsteps along the corridor outside. I could hear the door handle screech to open, but that corner of the room was not lit up enough for me to see who it was.

'Rosie.' My heart stopped when I recognized the voice. He walked toward me and removed the cloth from my mouth.

'Kai?' I said, confused.

'Yes,' he replied coldly.

'What's going on?' I asked, now knowing something definitely wasn't right.

'I thought you were a smart girl. No?' He frowned.

'It's just a formality, tying up some loose ends.' He walked back over to the steel table brushing his hands along the instruments that laid on top of it.

'What are you doing? Un-tie me,' I demanded.

'Now listen here, Rosie.' His voice started to rise. 'You talk only when spoken to, do you understand?'

I sucked in a breath, realising I had no way out of this. This was not a training exercise. I tried another failed attempt to free my hands.

'Now before I begin, I will allow questions.' He moved closer to me, his face almost touching mine as he lifted a stray hair that had fallen over my face and tucked it behind my ear, his hands rough against my skin. His touch sent another shiver down my spine and I felt bile rise up into my throat.

'Why are you doing this?'

'Because you are a daughter of the uprising. As Ezra is a son. You cannot live. Just like your parents before you, I will kill you both.' His eyes stared into mine as I felt his breath on my face.

'Ezra—' I gasped at the sound of his name.

'Yes, I'm afraid Ezra and the rest of your little group are dead.'

My chest tightened, 'You're lying.'

'I wish I was. I didn't care for the others but Ezra. He

was special. He was the best soldier I have seen in a long time, and his ability to heal could have been useful.' He sniffed, laughing through his nose. 'He's quite the fighter. Too bad he would never join Xavier. He could have put him to better use. If he hadn't of been so caught up with *you,* we might have had a chance.' He strode back toward the table pausing for a moment before lifting a long silver knife.

'You would never of had a chance,' I laughed at him, though I couldn't help my eyes starting to well up with tears, he can't be dead. Caleb, Grey, they all can't be dead.

'And you're lying, Ezra is going to come through that door and you'll regret this.' I couldn't think of anything else to say, I thought if I said those words, I might will it enough to come true.

'I'm going to enjoy this.' He stepped close to me again and I could feel his breath on my cheek.

'He is going to kill you,' I replied harshly. Rage flashed in his eyes before he lifted his hand and it connected with my jaw, jolting my head to the side. He grabbed my throat and clasped both hands tightly around it, I could feel the indentation his fingers were causing as my airway tightened. 'No. It won't be that easy. You're going to die slowly and painfully like your parents,' Kai responded with venom in his words. He released me and I breathed in, gasping for air. I spat out the blood that had gathered in my mouth from his punch.

'What about your wife?'

'My wife,' he stopped and smirked at me. 'My wife died for your parents because she was weak.'

'Is that why you joined Xavier?' I kept my eyes on the knife as he twisted it in his hand.

'Xavier's my father.' His grin grew wider as he looked at my reaction. I was in shock. Xavier was Kai's dad. His wife was part of the uprising and lost her life for it. Yet Kai had joined his father, why?

'Why ... Why didn't you fight for your world like your wife?'

'I think that's enough,' he walked closer, gripping the knife and pressing it against my chest just under my collarbone, I shuddered as the cold of the metal connected with my skin. He pushed down, hard. Slicing in a downward motion, I felt the instant burning and tearing and let out a muffled scream. He altered between his fists and the knife, as my clothes became stained red and the blood dripped to the floor. I could feel the room spinning around me, and my body became numb to the pain. I drifted in and out of consciousness and when I woke Kai's face would beam in delight, he was true to his word and was enjoying every moment of it. It continued in a vicious cycle for what seemed like hours. Kai walked back to the table and picked up a short hammer-like object with spikes protruding from its head, his lips pulled in a sick smile as he began walking slowly toward me, but he was interrupted by a loud knock on the door.

'What?' Kai yelled.

'You're needed sir, it's news about the base attack.' A man's voice exclaimed while entering the room, I recognized his voice but couldn't place a name. I was in too much pain to care to look up. Whoever it was wasn't here to rescue me. I coughed, spitting away the blood that had gathered in my mouth.

'I'll be back soon Rosie, don't you worry. We'll play with that next.' He set the weapon back down on the steel table making a loud clammer, then grabbed my chin roughly in his hand, forcing me to look at him.

'When I come back, I'll tell you all about Ezra's lifeless body,' he dropped my head from his grasp.

'You're pathetic,' I spat.

He placed the cloth back over my mouth and left, slamming the door behind him. I waited to hear his footsteps travel down the corridor before I tried with every bit of strength I could conjure to untie myself. It was useless, I could barely breathe, let alone untie myself, bile rose in my throat as a wave of nausea overtook me.

I heard a loud noise coming from the corridor, then the door handle slowly started to twist, this was it, Kai was coming back to finish what he had started. I watched the door closely, awaiting my fate. My heart quickened as I felt his presence when he entered the room. His steps drew closer and he came into view, I scanned from his legs to his face. Ezra. My body instantly relaxed at the sight of him, he was alive.

'Rosie.' He ran quickly to me, lifting the knife that was covered in my blood from the table and cutting me free.

He wrapped his arms around me, taking my weight as the rope dropped to the floor and into the pool of blood that had gathered there. He held me in his arms, removing the cloth that covered my mouth. I wrapped my arms around his neck as he scooped me up and carried me into the hallway, where Caleb and Greyson stood, both armed.

'We need to go now!' Greyson shouted, he glanced at me with a look of pain in his eyes.

Ezra ran holding me in his arms, taking us further down the corridor and through a small back door that led to a staircase. When we reached the top he pushed through another door, I felt the cool air wrap around me. We were outside, the jeep was waiting for us, lights on and still running. Caleb jumped into the driver's seat, Greyson beside him. Ezra **gently set** me in the backseat before getting in beside me. I could hear as bullets started cascading off the car.

'Go!' Greyson yelled at Caleb.

The tires spun on the gravel as Caleb picked up pace

'Where are we going?' Caleb asked once we reached a safe distance from the castle.

'There's a hotel not far from here, we can stay there for tonight, they won't find us there.' Ezra said, I rested my head on his shoulder as he looked down to me.

'How is she?' Caleb asked, concerned.

'Not good.' Ezra's voice was shaking. I've never heard

his voice sound like that before. He reached taking my hand in his, he was trying to heal me.

'Drive faster!' Greyson yelled at Caleb.

'I'm trying,' Caleb hissed at Greyson.

I could hear the worry in each of their voices as my eyes began to close.

Before I even opened my eyes, I could feel Ezra's warm body lying next to mine, his hand curled around mine.

'Hi beautiful.' His deep voice was gentle. Reassuring. I took a deep breath. I was safe. He was safe. They were safe.

'You're all ok?' I sighed in relief.

He nodded, 'We're all ok.' He smiled, trying to mask the worry in his voice.

'She's not healing, why isn't she healing?' Caleb paced the floor.

'I … I just need to sit up,' pain shot through every part of me at the simple movement. The numbness that I felt in the castle was gone and every part of me ached and throbbed. Almost as if it was happening all over again. I winced as I tried to lean myself up on my elbows, Ezra's arms wrapped around my waist supporting me.

'Rosie.' Was all he said, I could tell by his tone, something was wrong. Caleb said Ezra had been trying to heal me all night. It should have worked by now, the pain had dulled from the castle though not by much. Ezra's healing hadn't fully worked.

'No.' Greyson spoke, he moved from the end of the bed to stop me in my attempt to sit. I could feel Ezra's eyes glaring at him.

'What Greyson means is you need to rest.' Ezra's breath brushed against my neck, his hands still holding me.

'Is no one going to talk about the fact that she should be healed already? You've been trying to heal her all night now and she looks worse than she did when we took her from the castle, look how pale she is.' Caleb looked directly at me, his face showing the same pain and concern as the others.

'Does it usually take this long?' Greyson asked.

'No.'

'You have to try harder, you read that thing. You and Rosie together have more power than anyone from Atheria, that has to count for something right?' Caleb asked.

'It should have worked by now,' Ezra's words held a sharp tone, like he was saying one thing yet communicating another to Caleb. He looked to me and frowned. More power than anyone in Atheria, *together*. What did that mean? The sound of Ezra's voice broke my thoughts.

'Greyson, come here,' Ezra commanded.

Greyson moved to my side, taking over from where Ezra had been lying.

They each shared glances to each other, silent words passing by. My body began to shake, the coldness prickled my skin. Caleb started pacing along the room again. Ezra took my hand in his, closing his eyes. I don't think I would ever get used to the feel of his skin against mine.

Sharp pain travelled throughout my body, coursing through my veins stinging me like venom as it moved in waves, before forcing its way out from the tips of my fingers and into the hand Ezra was holding. The pain was excruciating, stinging me like a hot branding iron connecting with bare skin. When it reached Ezra's hand it disappeared like it had never existed.

I gasped, turning my head into Greyson's chest and

tugging on his shirt as each wave of pain came and left my body. I felt the colour return to my face, my bones move back into place, my cuts knit together. I looked at Ezra, who was still gripping my hand tightly. His eyes were still closed, and he was grimacing as he felt every wave of pain. He could feel it as I had. He was taking my pain for me. As the last of the pain left my body and entered his, he let go of my hand and opened his eyes.

'How do you feel Rosie?' he asked breathless. I smiled gently at him I started to sit up, Greyson's hand supporting my back. Caleb rushed over and took my hand helping me to my feet. Ezra was clearly exhausted from taking my pain and slumped down on the bed in front of where I now stood, Caleb cautiously supporting some of my weight.

'I feel … great.' I smiled at Ezra and rested my hand on his cheek. 'How are *you* feeling?'

'I'll be fine,' he responded. I could see the pain he was in, but he was being typical Ezra and brushing it off. His ability worked like my projection, the longer it took him to heal someone the more exhausted he got.

'Why did it take so long for you to heal me?' I asked, looking around at all three of them.

'We're not sure,' Caleb responded, his eyebrows narrowed lost in thought.

I sat back down beside Ezra he lifted his arm and placed it around my back, holding me close to him and placing a tender kiss on my forehead. It was only then I looked around the room and took in my surroundings. I realised where we were and let out a soft chuckle.

'What is it?' Ezra asked, looking at me suspiciously.

'Of all the hotels, you took us to Dawn's?' I smiled.

He looked at me and started laughing, 'It's tradition now.'

We laid down on the tacky bed for the second time in our lives as I curled into him.

'Get some sleep you two. Grey and I will keep watch till morning and then we are out of *here*.' Caleb looked around, disgusted.

I leant up to kiss Ezra and held my hand on his cheek, tracing his scar with my finger. 'I thought you were dead,' I said, a tear slipping away from me.

'I'd never leave you,' he said as he leaned down to kiss me.

Chapter 23

'We need to get out of here now!' Caleb shouted.

'What's wrong?' Ezra jumped up to sit.

'There's some crazy woman cursing out Grey right now for overstaying. She's already made a few suggesting comments that I'd rather not repeat.' He looked at us sheepishly.

'Dawn,' Ezra and I both said together, and Caleb gave us a strange look.

We both stood up putting our shoes on. I didn't even bother looking in the mirror; I didn't want to see what I looked like. Blood had stained my clothing and my hair. It was lucky the sheets in here were red. Ezra's shirt was smeared with blood like my own clothing, a shiver ran down my spine at the memory of last night. I held Ezra's hand as we left Dawn's hotel room in search for Greyson. It didn't take long for us to find her, standing at her reception desk mouthing something we couldn't hear to Grey who looked like he wanted the ground to swallow him up. As we approached them her eyes glazed over to Ezra and then to me.

'You,' she said, glaring at Ezra.

Greyson let out a sigh, glad the attention was now off him.

'It was a pleasure as always, Dawn,' Ezra replied sarcastically.

Dawn scowled at him and turned to me, 'And you,' she said, giving me a disgusted look. I couldn't help but let out a small chuckle. What this woman must think, if only she knew the truth.

'I'm sure we'll be back,' I grinned. I moved my arm around Ezra's back as we turned our bodies away from Dawn's walking out to the carpark. He placed a light kiss on the top of my head.

It didn't take long before we reached Caspian's base. It was the only place Ezra was sure we could go. We had no idea what lies Kai might have spread about us by now, if any at all. We couldn't take the risk, we had to go to the only person we could trust. And even that wasn't certain.

As we walked inside Caspian's base, the room fell silent. Six of Caspian's crew strode toward us, angry expressions panned their faces as they raised their weapons. The rest of his team watched on with baited breath.

'Stop right there.' Caspian's voice cut through the silence. He walked over to us with a look of confusion.

'We need to talk in private,' Caspian lowered his voice.

'I'll take it from here,' he turned and addressed the six men and women glaring daggers at us, as they followed his command and lowered their weapons. They didn't question him, at least not verbally, but it was clear they were hesitant.

He glanced to my blood-stained clothing and gave me a strange look. We followed him as he led us to the back of the warehouse and through a door leading into a small office. There were cases and cases of literature piled high on three tall bookcases and one small dusty window, this room, unlike Kai's, had a desk and chair with more papers sprawled across it.

'What the hell is going on?' Caspian looked directly at Ezra.

'Do you know about Kai?' Ezra asked.

'He called me telling me you and Rosie had joined Xavier and took Caleb and Greyson with you,' he glared at Ezra.

'*He's* the traitor,' Ezra's voice sounded agitated.

Caspian looked at Ezra and then around at us letting out a frustrated sigh. 'I have a room of people out there that think otherwise. We have orders to kill you on sight.'

'Show him the necklace,' Caleb spoke.

Ezra reached into his pocket and pulled out the gold chain with two stones entwined together, a sapphire and an emerald, the boys had filled me in on the car journey. I still had so many questions.

Caspian touched the stones and the hologram appeared. Pages of Ezra's mother's handwriting, detailing the rebellion and Xavier's plans. Everything she could possibly have known. She shared strategies they had tried, and failed, information about our abilities and the founding families and then a photo. Caspian let out an audible gasp as he looked at it. It was a photo of Xavier, standing next to a woman and beneath them, a child, Kai.

'Kai is Xavier's son,' Caspian concluded.

'That's not all, he's working with him,' Ezra paused. 'That night we came here to protect our weaponry, it was Kai who told them where they were kept.'

'I can't believe this,' Caspian said, running his fingers through his dark hair and disheveling it slightly. 'We have to let the others know.' He paused and looked at me again, 'What happened to you?' his voice seeped with concerned as he looked me over, taking in my undoubtably horrific state.

'Kai,' was all I could say. I couldn't even let myself think about what had just happened to me. Caspian seemed to understand and nodded empathetically, not pushing me any further. Ezra squeezed my hand and then let Caspian, who was still holding the necklace, lead the way.

After hours of explaining to Caspian's team there were still a few people that were apprehensive to believe us, but Caspian was quick to silence them. We knew we were going to have to contact the other bases and explain everything to them, hoping they would join us. Otherwise, with our lack of numbers we didn't stand a chance against Xavier or Kai.

I stopped Caspian as he walked past me, 'Have you got a shower?'

He chuckled, 'of course we have a shower.'

'Come on,' he nudged his head for me to follow. 'You can use mine, the water's hot.' He stopped and looked over his shoulder, lowering his voice to a whisper, 'don't tell the other's that though.' He smirked.

'You're secrets safe with me.' I smiled back, glad we had at least one alley with a loyal team.

Caspian showed me to the shower and kindly gathered some clothing for me to change into. He had given the boys each a change of clothing as well, we all needed it. I closed the door from the small shower room and entered into Caspian's own quarters, drying the rest of my hair with the towel. He had a quaint room beside his office with a small single bed placed underneath another dusty window, my change of clothes lay on top of the burgundy sheets. As I pulled my top over my head, I caught a glimpse of myself in the mirror that rested against the wall. My hands rose automatically to trace the red scarring beneath my collar bone. I didn't even want to look at the rest. Ezra knocked lightly before entering, and when he looked at me, I could tell he knew exactly what I was thinking. My hand still rested on the scar and I felt disgusted that Kai had marked me. He walked in and closed the door tightly behind him. I gave a slight smile, but I couldn't hide my feelings from him.

'Rosie, it's ok.' He looked at me the same way Caspian did, like he understood exactly how I felt. Of course he understood, he went through this for years and my chest tightened at the realisation of how long he had suffered. He walked over and placed his hand on top of mine, his thumb smoothing along the redness of my scar. I moved my hand to hold his and reached it up to my lips, placing a soft kiss onto his skin. I moved into him, placing my head against his chest as he covered me with his arms.

'Have you read this?' I asked Ezra.

We were sitting outside on the rocks that lined the pebbled shore beside the lake. Greyson and Caleb were skimming stones in front of us as I held the necklace, reading through each page of information. Ezra sat nestled beside me, taking in as much as he could. None of us had had a proper chance to study it yet and with each page I turned, the more I learned about Atheria. There was so much that we didn't know.

'Briefly,' Ezra said, moving closer to get a better view of the page I was on.

'When our families link that is when we are strongest. It's only happened once before ...'

'Us,' he spoke.

'That's why my parents and yours wanted to send both of us to Earth, when we are together our abilities are enhanced. That's why I can sense when you enter a room and feel your emotions.'

'I always thought it was just another ability we had that we shared.'

'Xavier must know.' That's why they separated us, so we would be easier to kill.

Ezra moved his arm around me, 'He's not going to win.'

'No, he's not,' I vowed.

'Damn right he's not,' Caleb turned to us grinning, 'and I'll take great pleasure in it.'

'None of this explains why it took so long for you to heal me though,' I sighed, placing the necklace back over my head and sealing its contents. We needed to know if something was wrong. If we entered a battle with Xavier and Kai and Ezra couldn't heal us quick enough, it could be deadly.

'That would be because of this,' Caspian spoke from behind us. He was holding a small journal illustrated with an image of a vial containing what looked like some sort of liquid.

'What's that?' Grey asked.

'*Mors*,' Caspian answered. 'It was used to torture prisoners many, many years ago. When Ezra mentioned he wasn't able to heal you, I remembered my grandfather telling me about this. I had to go and check in one of his old journals before I could be sure.'

'But I didn't see Kai with that.'

'All he would need to do is put it on his hands or

weaponry, it makes our bodies unable to react to cuts and injuries. Even with Ezra's ability to heal, it forces it to take longer.' He walked over, taking a seat on a rock beside Ezra and passed him the journal. Ezra took it examining it, it didn't look like anything special but from what Caspian had just said it was certainly powerful. It had taken Ezra hours to heal me, when usually it would have been minutes, depending on the injury.

'If Kai uses this on his weapons ...' I was worried. If Kai used that on his weapons it would weaken us. There was no way Ezra could heal everyone. His chances before of healing everyone had been slim, but now with it taking longer, it was going to be next to impossible. If two of us got hit at the same time – that thought doesn't even bear thinking about.

'We need a plan,' Caleb sounded uneasy.

Ezra and Caspian nodded, we stood up and followed him inside and into another room with an extremely large oval table. His team filled in behind us each taking a seat. As we went to take our seats Caspian lightly nudged my arm and nodded to Ezra, gesturing for us to stand beside him. Caleb and Grey sat down as we stood at the top of the table.

'There's word that Xavier has taken over the castle,'

Caspian addressed his team.

'Well, there goes the plan to take Kai down first,' Greyson spoke.

'It'll be harder getting into the castle but if we can get to them both at the same time—' Ezra said.

'We can end this,' I finished, and he nodded.

We spent hours going over and over our strategy. Our plan was solid, well, as solid as it could be. We had some of the other bases on our side now too, but others were still hesitant to believe us over Kai. If Kai was willing to use *Mors*, what other measures would he go to? I shuddered at the very thought, I knew all too well how sick and twisted Kai could be.

Ezra and I took to a quiet corner of the warehouse, we wanted to see how much we really did affect each other's abilities. After a few hours we realised that we didn't need to be standing directly beside each other or even touching each other for our abilities to be enhanced, although it did help. Just being in the same room together was enough, but when we couldn't see each other our abilities weakened. That explained why when I projected alone, I could never stay in them for as long as I could when Ezra was with me.

'I need to speak with you both.' Caspian spoke from behind me, his voice held a certain urgency I hadn't heard from him before.

'What's wrong?' Ezra moved beside me, we were far enough away that no one else would hear our conversation.

'I searched through my grandfather's journals and there's an antidote for *Mors*,' he cleared his throat, 'it's called *Sano*.'

'Have we got it here?' I asked my hopes rising. A cure was exactly what we needed.

'Yes, but we only have enough for a small vile.' Caspian looked to Ezra.

'It'll have to do we'll use it sparsely only on those that would die without.' Ezra seemed torn by this decision, the *Mors* will still weaken us if they use it, the promise of saving everyone had now disappeared.

We sat around the picnic tables outside the warehouse, the warm glow from the lights glistened down on us as we ate, going from moments of laughter to solace. Tomorrow was the day we would fight. We had acquired more now than we began our day with, I only hoped it would be enough. I fell asleep in Ezra's arms that night, listening to his breathing and feeling his breath against my ear, his warmth surrounded me, and I longed for this war to be over.

Chapter 24

As we packed the jeep full of weapons, the atmosphere around us was tense. We went over our plan with Caspian and his team one last time before getting into Ezra's jeep and heading for the castle. I sat in the passenger seat with Ezra's hand resting in mine as he drove, glancing down at me occasionally with a smile. Caleb and Greyson were chatting in the backseat and for a moment you would have thought we were going on a road trip, how I wished that were true.

We pulled up to the main road before the turn into the castle and Ezra parked off-road. This was it. Our plan was either going to work or … No. I can't think like that. We walked through the forest as the castle came into sight. I could feel a pull in my stomach as I thought again what Kai was capable of, then I felt a warm hand touch mine, I forgot he could feel my emotions.

'Ready?' Caleb turned to Ezra, who nodded, squeezing my hand one last time, then moved from my side to Caleb's. They were no longer protected by the cover of the trees. I stood next to Greyson as I watched them both disappear, feeling my heart tug in my chest after them.

'This is going to work Rosie,' Grey gave me a reassuring smile.

'What if Caspian doesn't get there in time?' I said, worried.

'He'll be there,' he said in a tone that was both serious and comforting.

Every moment that passed I felt more and more afraid something had happened. Something that wasn't planned. Greyson tried to distract me, talking about memories from our past. I appreciated him trying to keep the mood light, but it was next to impossible for me to think about anything else. I tried to focus on how my body felt, trying to sense if he was still ok. I couldn't feel anything, I hoped that was a good sign. My eyes drifted up the length of the trees, to the sky. The branches reached for each other unable to touch, as a sliver of light forced its way through.

Caleb came crashing through the cover of the forest. 'Let's go,' he said in a hurried tone. Without any questions we picked up our weapons and followed him toward the castle, paying careful attention to follow his footsteps exactly. We stood beside the stone wall, each of us took turns and climbed to the second floor making our way through an open window. Caleb jumped in first, holding out his hand for me to take. Once my feet hit the floor, I saw Ezra and sighed in relief.

'We need to get to the next floor,' Ezra looked at me, giving me a soft smile before turning to the door and peering into the hallway.

'Let's go,' he instructed.

We followed him down the corridor and up the staircase. I knew Liam and Knox's room was on this floor, I had walked by their room many times on my way to the fourth floor where our suite was. We heard footsteps and I immediately opened Liam and Knox's door, ushering them inside.

'What are you doing in here?' Knox said with a stern look.

'What are *you* doing here? Everyone's in the main hall,' Caleb asked.

'A few of us stayed in our rooms,' he glared at Caleb.

'Is Liam down there?' I asked, looking around to see no sign of him, other than his clothes flung across his bed. It was a stark contrast to Knox's side of the room. His bed was neatly made with a stack of books resting on the nightstand.

'Liam's dead,' his words harsh as he stared at me, his eyes fueled with anger.

'What—' What did he mean Liam was dead? Kai told Ezra he had released him.

'Kai thought he was the traitor when it was really *you*,' he started to raise his voice.

'We aren't the traitors Knox, Kai is,' I spoke back to him. I was hurt that he would think any of us were traitors and that I had any role to play in Liam's death. Liam's *death*. My mind suddenly shot back to the room Kai had me in, and the blood that stained the floor. Was that Liam's blood? I shuddered at the thought.

'K … Kai?' he stuttered.

'Yes man. Kai! Now that we've done our little reunion,

can we get going? We are kind of in the middle of something here if you hadn't noticed, Caleb snapped.

Knox stood up, grabbing a gun from underneath his bed, I'm not even going to ask. He followed us into the hallway. We were going to Kai's office. We wanted to take them both down with as few casualties as possible. Caspian was to keep them busy until we got there, then he would follow them back to Kai's office where we would be waiting.

We made it to the fifth floor and standing outside Kai's office were the two usual guards. We stopped.

'Something isn't right,' Ezra said as he frowned.

The men eyed Ezra and glanced at the rest of us, clocking our weapons and raising their own defensively. Laughter sounded from behind us, as we turned on our heels.

'Xavier,' Ezra clenched his jaw. This *was* Xavier. I had seen this man before, I was certain. He was tall with jet black hair and even darker eyes. This was the man that had been in the restaurant weeks ago.

'You really thought it would be this easy,' his laughter echoed throughout the hallway. I could feel the hairs on the back of my neck stand up. Ezra moved his hand to my back in a comforting way. He could sense I had tensed, and

I could feel the anger radiating from him. Ezra wasn't scared like me, he was livid.

Our attention quickly turned in front of us again as Kai appeared, his men holding Caspian, who had bruises and cuts covering his face and was barely able to stand on his own. A smug look covered Kai's face, as though he had already won.

'Rosie. So good to see you're still alive,' Kai spoke in an eerily gentle tone. I felt Ezra's grip on me tighten, his anger now refocused on Kai.

'Well, isn't this a great reunion?' Xavier hissed, appearing behind him now were more of his men.

'If you would shut your mouth it would be even better,' Caleb sneered at him, he was uncharacteristically tense.

Xavier laughed, a deep wicked laugh.

'Kill him.' He ordered his men with a raise of his hand, and before any of us could react, a shot fired, and Caleb fell to his knees. Ezra and I rushed beside him, blood soaking through his clothing. The bullet had gone through his right shoulder. Grey and Knox raised their weapons and stood in front to shield us, as Xavier and Kai stayed completely still, watching. Kai waved his hand and his men stepped slowly toward us. Thuds of footsteps echoed down the hallway, I recognized each of them as they approached and collided with Xavier's men. Our back up.

My hands were shaking as I looked at Caleb struggling to breathe. He was barely healing. They had laced the bullets. Ezra held his hand his grasp was tight the white of his knuckles showing. I opened the ointment, *Sano*. It countered the effects of the *Mors*. I looked into his eyes, hoping he could heal him quicker this time with the help of the *Sano*, but then his eyes left mine, glancing behind me and I could sense his fear.

'Rosie!' Ezra shouted.

I turned just in time to dodge a punch from Kai. Caspian lay unconscious behind him and Kai's men had moved to fight more of ours. Bodies were dropping and I couldn't tell who was winning, if anyone. Kai had grabbed my arm, his long fingers pressed tightly against my skin. He glanced down for a moment to lift a knife from his pocket, I took the opportunity and threw a punch that connected with his jaw, his hands released me long enough for me to knock the knife from him. I looked over quickly to Caleb and then Ezra. There was no movement from Caleb and

Ezra's eyes were following me. Kai pulled me in again, this time wrapping his arms around my throat, his grasp was tight and his face was close to mine. His eyes had grown dark. I clawed at his hands to try to get a breath, but his hold was too strong. Hoping for a distraction I projected us back to Atheria. Kai was stunned, as he studied the scene. The same scene I had first shown everyone in the training gym, the beach. I raised my gun, aiming at him and pulled the trigger without hesitation. I ended the projection, I wanted him to die alone in a cold hallway, not surrounded by the beauty of Atheria. Kai dropped onto the stone flooring as he gasped for air. I watched as he took his final breath. If I had of had the chance, I would have made his death slower, more painful for all he had done, he got more than he deserved. I felt a hold on my arm and turned to defend myself, stopping when I recognized who it was, Greyson.

'You ok?' he asked. I nodded.

'Caleb!' I yelled as I ran over to him, his eyes had now opened.

'I'm good, someone get me a gun,' he said, pulling me into a quick hug. Ezra slumped down next to him, he was exhausted, I could feel it. Greyson passed Caleb a gun and helped him to his feet, he glanced over at Kai's lifeless body and gave me a sly grin. Our short embrace lasted seconds, as more of Xavier's men pulled us back into the fight. I reached for Ezra's hand, helping him up. He was too easy a target sitting, his legs buckled underneath him as I pushed him back against the wall to steady him.

I clasped his hand tightly, trying and not really having any idea what I was doing. We were meant to have some sort of connection that helped strengthen each other. Ezra's ability was to heal and we needed that right now. I felt a sensation almost like an electric shock course through my body and into Ezra's. In that moment he was able to stand on his own. His hands twisted around my hair as he looked into my eyes and then in an instant everything changed, we were surrounded. I fought a girl about my age and a boy younger than me, I pushed my knife into the girl's chest taking her life. I didn't feel at all how I felt when I took Kai's life. It was different. Kai had deserved to die, but this girl and boy, they were caught up in a war that they probably didn't even understand themselves.

We fought beside Greyson, Caleb and the rest of our men and women, they had come from all the other bases and I could see some familiar faces from the castle fighting with us too. Xavier had come back into view and was casually walking through the chaos, his eyes fixated on Ezra. I pulled my knife from another of Xavier's men, when yet another came toward me. I tried to put away the sick feeling in my gut as I took life after life, it was them or us.

Ezra and Xavier had reached each other and were throwing punch after punch, Ezra seemed to have the upper hand. Each time I had a slight break my eyes immediately went to him. I could feel how furious he was, it was coursing through my veins as well. I tried moving closer to them, but two men stood blocking my way. Greyson pulled one away from me, shooting him and I watched Xavier and Ezra. Xavier had a gun in his back pocket, his hand was reaching for it as two men held Ezra. I turned to look at Greyson, but he was no longer beside me. Another man was charging toward me and as I shot him and he hit the ground, I heard another shot fire from where Ezra and Xavier were standing. Ezra had a gun in his hand, and the two men that had been beside him were dead. I gasped at what I saw next. Greyson fell at the same time as Xavier.

'Greyson!' I screamed.

I ran to him, fighting through the chaos. I reached out to grab his hand and as I looked down, there was blood, everywhere. I searched his body for the wound. His breathing was slowing, and his breaths were becoming shorter and more infrequent. Ezra knelt beside us, taking Grey's other hand.

'It's ok Grey, you're going to be ok,' I said, moving my hand along his forehead, he reached out and held tightly on to my hand. I looked up to Ezra who was deep in concentration.

'I …' he started, but couldn't get the words out.

'It's ok, you don't have to talk. Save your energy,' I smiled reassuringly at him. I felt a sudden surge of fear from Ezra and as I looked over to him, I could see his chest rising and lowering in a panicked movement.

'What's wrong?' I asked, my heartbeat increasing as I took in his expression.

'He's …' he paused, struggling to get the words out, 'He's not healing Rosie, it isn't working.'

'What do you mean it's not working? It worked with Caleb,' I screamed, tears started uncontrollably running down my face. Greyson took his hand from my grasp and gently started wiping them away, smiling softly at me.

Ezra closed his eyes and held Greyson's hand tighter, he was trying to concentrate more.

'Rosie,' Grey spoke clearly now, looking into my eyes.

'No,' I shook my head, 'don't you dare.' I raised my hand resting it on his cheek. 'You're going to be *fine.*' My voice broke on the last word as more tears escaped, streaming down my face.

The edges of his lips turned upward into a slight smile. 'I'm glad I met you Rosie,' he said softly, his hand still resting on my cheek.

'Stop. Please Grey, this isn't it. This isn't happening. I told you. You're going to be fine,' I said in desperation.

'Ezra!' I yelled. He opened his eyes and looked at me in a way I will never forget. I shook my head at him. 'Try again,' I screamed. He took Greyson's hand again, but Caleb reached in and broke his connection.

'What are you doing Caleb?' I sneered at him.

'Rosie, it's not working,' he rested his hand on my shoulder trying to comfort me, as tears welled in his own eyes.

As I looked down to Greyson my heart felt like it was

being torn from my chest. I projected us back to the cabin, on that little day bed, when we were happy. Greyson's eyes fluttered around as he recognized where we were, and his lips curled upwards in a smile.

'Rosie,' Greyson spoke again and I shook my head at him.

'It's ok,' he closed his eyes and the life drained from him. I could feel his body go limp and his hand collapsed from my cheek to his side. My projection ended as I broke down, Ezra moved to me, pulling me into his chest. I resisted him at first and then relaxed into his embrace. We stayed there for as long as we could before Ezra pulled me to stand. When I finally looked up, all the fighting had ceased, Xaviers men had retreated. I glanced at where Xavier's body had been, he was gone.

'Where's Xavier?' I sniffed.

Caleb and Ezra shifted their eyes from me to the empty space where Xavier had been shot. They looked at each other and then to me as concern covered every inch of their expressions. I went to hold onto the necklace, fumbling when I realised it was no longer there.

'Ezra,' he looked down to meet my eyes, his arms were still clutched tightly around me.

'The necklace, it's gone,' he glanced down to my neck.

'Find Xavier!' Ezra commanded to the men and women left in front of us, who began searching the castle.

Hours passed and there was still no sign of Xavier or the necklace. We stood in the main hall with Caspian, Caleb, and a few of the leaders from the other bases. Xavier was gone and so was the necklace containing every bit of inside information he would ever need to take down Atheria. The room was tense and all I could think about was Greyson's lifeless body. I stood still as I watched Caspian, Caleb, Ezra and the other leaders discuss and devise the next plan. Ezra kept glancing to me with looks of concern. Xavier was now an even larger threat. I was wrong before, we hadn't won anything. But I knew I would kill Xavier, and it wouldn't be the quick death Kai had enjoyed. Any guilt I had felt from killing Xavier's army had disappeared and been replaced with a rage I had never felt before. I needed to end this.

Ezra walked over to me taking my hand in his, I softened slightly at his touch, he leant in placing a gentle kiss on my cheek, 'I'm sorry,' he said, looking down and not meeting my eyes.

'It wasn't your fault.'

'I couldn't save him,' he answered, his voice sounded broken.

'I don't blame you,' I said, trying to comfort him, I could feel his guilt.

'I mean it, you did everything you could Ezra.' His eyes met mine and I leant up, placing my lips softly onto his as he deepened our kiss.

I knew joining this fight would most likely mean loss, and I knew I had been naïve to think that that loss wouldn't directly affect me. Greyson had died today, that moment would remain with me for the rest of my life. I knew what I had to do, I would stop at nothing to watch Xavier's body turn cold, and I would enjoy it.

Thank you so much for reading. If you enjoyed *The Worlds That Separated Us*, please consider leaving an honest review with your favourite store.

ACKNOWLEDGEMENTS

I really do have so many people to thank that helped me in this process. I want to start by thanking my husband for always supporting me and my dreams. Without your constant encouragement none of this would have been possible. You helped me through late nights and many, many cups of coffee to help turn this dream of mine into a reality. When I would doubt myself and my capability, you were always there talking sense into me just when I needed it and cheered me on, for that I will never stop thanking you.

My dad for giving me the best advice, to never let fear stand in the way of my ambitions. That has stayed with me throughout this entire process and for that I am so grateful, thanks daddy! My mum who has always been there supporting me my whole life, through everything. You'll never know how much your support means to me.

To my extremely talented book cover designer Mandi

Lynn from Stonebridge books. Thank you for bringing my vision to life, It's absolutely perfect and I love it!

My equally as talented editor Hannah Sears. Thank you for helping me tell my story in the best way possible. Your help and guidance were invaluable to me.

To my two children Lily and Jack, who inspire me every day to never let go of my imagination. My sisters Sarah and Naomi, my best friend in the entire world Hannah and the rest of my family and friend's you guys are the absolute best. I'm so blessed to have so many supportive people in my life, cheering me on and always without fail being there for me when I need it the most. I really am surrounded by some of the best people in this world and not a day goes by where I'm not thankful for those blessings in my life. You guys I love you all, even more than chocolate!

Lastly but certainly not least, to my readers. Thank you from the bottom of my heart for reading my book. It means more to me than you will ever know. I hope you enjoyed Rosie's story just as much as I enjoyed writing it.